Book 1
Chronicals of th... ...

The
War Ender's
Apprentice

Written by
Elizabeth Guizzetti

Edited by Joe Dacy
Cover and Interior Illustrations by Elizabeth Guizzetti

This is a work of fiction. Names, characters, businesses, places, events and incidents are products of the author's imagination or used in a fictitious manner. Any resemblance to actual persons, living or dead, or actual events is purely coincidental. (Also weird. I mean really this book is about a group of elves.)

Printed in the United States of America

Paperback ISBN-13: 978-0-9995598-0-2
EBook ISBN-13: 978-0-9995598-1-9

Library of Congress Control Number: 2017916822

Dedicated to Nikki

Seven Populated Realms protected by the Guild

Cannik (Can nik)
Watery Realm of the vodnik

Daouail (Da o wail)
Realm of the Daosith

Dynion (Di nee on)
Realm of the humans

Fatidel (Fat i del)
Realm of the Fates

Fairhdel (Fair del)
Realm of the Fairsinge

Larcia (Lar see a)
Realm of the dwarves

Si Na (See Na)
Realm of the telchine
*Uttalassus (Ut ta lass us)
Technically within the Realm of Si Na.
Land of the gnomes

Realms not within the Guild

Risford (Rise Ford)
Realm of the Giants

Widae (Wed ae)
Realm of Dragons

Uncharted Realms

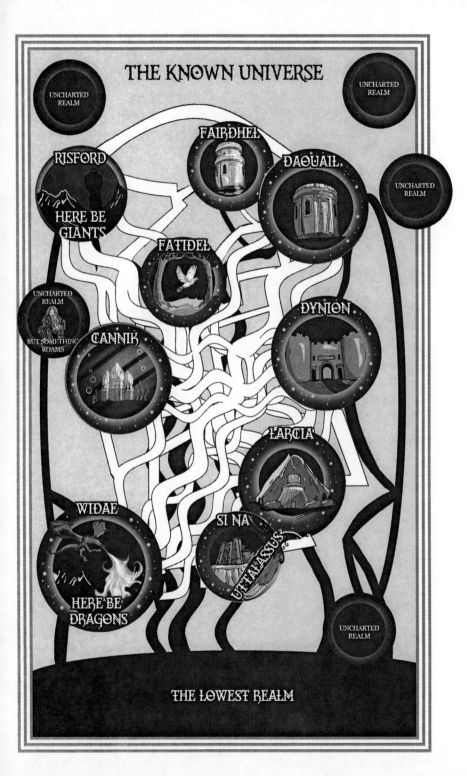

The
War Ender's
Apprentice

Chapter 1
An unnamed beach
at the edge of Daouail

A DARK SPLOTCH BLEMISHED THE CLEAR blue sky over the deep ocean. In seconds, wind and waves rose from the previously calm water. With an ear-piercing snap, the atmosphere tore open, exposing a vortex absent of light, pulling water towards it.

Shimmering plates of honeycombed glass held with golden hinges encased the Interrealm vessel's massive wooden hull and decking as it glided into the sea. The vortex closed, leaving only clear sky and calm sea.

Aboard, the crew scurried to unfold the enclosures to allow in the sweetness of fresh air and adjust the sails for Daouail's gentle wind and currents. They settled in a north by northeast direction.

Leagues away, obscured among tangled driftwood, Lady Alana Martlet of House Eyreid peered through her eyeglass. She focused on the movements of the crew. Taxonomic differences aside, they all looked too gaunt for health. Their movements were practiced, but slow as they led a small party of chained slaves to the uppermost deck and threw buckets of seawater on them. Shivering in the wind, several of the elfkin slaves bore the tri-pointed ears of her people. She smiled. *Now I have an excuse ...*

Munitions covered the ship bow to stern, but this far from port, security was lax. Towards the bow, a Daosith overseer stood guard, whip in hand. Two more humans and a Daosith clustered around the wheel of the aftmost deck. From her dossier, she identified the human captain and the Daosith purser. Once the course was set, a human, a telchine, and two Daosith cooked greasy pottage of unidentified ingredients in huge kettles near the center of the weather deck where five smaller boats were tethered. Those might be useful.

Alana pocketed her eyeglass. "I count eight. We can handle them easily enough."

Roark's young delicate profile stiffened as if it was a piece carved ivory. Though her nephew and apprentice didn't lower his eyeglass, his high brow knotted in a scowl. "Aren't you worried about a complaint?"

She snapped open a boiled leather pouch on her belt and removed an etched bone compact with three dials: for the Realm, for the number of moons, and for their phases. Once the compact flipped open, a barometer measured atmospheric pressure, and tiny copper flags indicated wind direction, speed, and the Realm's major natural light sources to calculate the placement of the deepest shadows. She pointed at their map. "We should head in through the east. Clouds should roll in about a half-hour."

"I have to swim around the whole boat? Are you sure you don't just want to kill the captain and purser as contracted?"

"Number of people I kill doesn't change the distance you must swim."

"All eight isn't the job."

She pointed towards the limestone cliffs where the seabirds nested among the grasses and spruce. "We should set back to the next beach over. Those hills have an easier incline."

"Freeing slaves isn't the job," Roark said.

"Move fast and quiet."

"I know the plan, but it's not the job," he repeated. "Corwin..."

"I'll deal with him. Become a shadow."

Roark turned away and removed his overtunic.

Alana dressed in the weave. The black fabric was created for ease of movement and silence once it hugged the skin. She tightened her scabbards and applied greasepaint around her eyes. Her final touch was to tie two tarred sacks on her belt. The larger was needed for the job, and the other held a day's ration of hardtack and enough coin to make it to the nearest Guild house — just in case the job went bad.

Afterwards, she inspected Roark for any flash of color, pale skin or loose weaponry within the black. She thought and let her pride wash over him: Your attention to detail is improving.

Roark smiled at the compliment and rechecked her gear both for instruction and good sense. "Nothing's out of place, except your mind."

"When I was your age, apprentices respected their masters," Alana lied.

*

CLOUDS ROLLED IN, CASTING THE REALM IN deep shadows. The last sun dipped into the ocean. They pushed away from the shore on an unlit boat painted black as pitch. The sea was calm enough for Alana to steer the rudder and Roark to row without hindrance until they drifted into the current behind the larger ship.

At twenty-five paces, they dove into the water with

a length of rope. As instructed, Roark carefully tethered the rowboat to the stern. Alana edged along the wooden hull. Wearing spiked gloves, she climbed to the upper deck.

Goddess, it stinks. A horrid mix of feces, bodily odors, vomit, blood and greasy pottage filled her nostrils. Over the hatchway stood the overseer holding a scourge of nine twisted thongs. His ill-fitted, ragged clothes looked as if they might rip any moment. His white hair was cropped short, but unwashed and ashy patches of skin flaked off his knees and elbows. She might have felt pity. However, a slave's moan sang out into the air; the overseer hit his whip upon the grating. His eyes expressed eagerness to apply it upon the flesh of his victims.

Alana's deceased aunt reminded her conscience, "We don't kill for vengeance, Alana Mira Eyreid." But her mentor was dead; she was the Guild Master now.

Alana slid to the deck, removed her metal spikes, hid them in a lifeboat and waited for Roark's signal. He slipped aft to find the purser. Alana crawled into the captain's night compartment — a dank, private room one deck below.

In the dim twilight, Alana observed an emaciated Fairsinge woman loosely chained to the wall. Her neck was restrained by a tight iron collar. Her once smooth white cheek branded and ebony hair cropped to her scalp. Upon closer inspection, her body did not look as fully formed as a woman's, but Alana did not know if that was malnutrition or age. Her eyes were crusted with dried tears, and her reddened nose had left a trail of snot to her mouth.

Knowing the sheer stupidity of such an action, Alana knelt before her and pulled off her face mask and exposed her three-pointed ear.

A hint of life came back into the girl's eyes.

"You must be quiet and hide."

The girl mumbled and nodded in agreement.

Alana picked the lock. Once freed, the girl scampered to the far corner and pressed her branded face into her hands.

Replacing her mask, Alana glanced in the dirty mirror to ensure her auburn and silver hair was still covered.

As her dossier said was his habit, at eight bells, the captain entered alone. He undressed. Ribs and knobby joints were stretched across his mottled flesh.

He pulled at the girl's chain. Holding the other end, Alana leapt from the shadows.

His last words were: "What in the devil?"

She tackled him and clamped his ankle in the iron, then shoved a dirty sock in his mouth. Alana could have killed him quickly. Instead, she pierced one lung and let him gasp.

Alana knelt on his chest and whispered, "You should not brag you don't pay your debts, Captain. The Guild does not allow malingerers to engage in Interrealm travel. It's bad for business."

Alana grabbed his wrist and, using her saber, chopped off his hand which she placed in a tarred sack on her belt. Bleeding and gasping, the captain clutched his stump closer to his chest as she stood.

She opened his desk and found a small box of coin, though not nearly the amount needed for the debt. She opened the ledger. *Damn me to the lowest Realm!*

Her dossier had suggested the northernmost port in Daouail would be the ship's first stop for the arena trade. Unfortunately, the ship landed in Dynion's Port Denwort where several children, aged ten to thirteen, had been sold as house slaves. She pressed her hand to the ledger. Unsure if she would ever be able to right the wrong, she ripped out the page and shoved it in her emergency sack.

She unlocked the captain's sea chest and dug for money and other valuables. She found a vial of perfume from the Fairhdel province of the same name, but little else.

"No wonder they made an early stop. The ne'er do well probably holds a debt in every Realm." May he be resurrected as a toad.

Alana threw the branded girl a linen shirt from the chest and a wool blanket off the captain's berth. The girl didn't respond, even as the fabric landed on her.

Pressing her finger to the girl's lips, Alana tried to prod her out of the corner. The girl was frozen. Alana put the linen shirt over her head and covered her in the woolen blanket. She still didn't budge.

Alana stomped on the captain's torso. She punctured his other lung and scabbarded her blade. With the hope his gasping was gratifying to the girl, Alana hoisted her up in her arms. In seconds, the dead weight aggrieved her aging shoulders, but she crept up the ladder and sternwards to the first of the four lifeboats without fail.

"Hide here until we free the others."

Shivering, the girl lay at the bottom of the boat, covered in the woolen blanket.

Moving silently, Alana redrew her saber and slid behind the overseer. Seeking a faster death than the one she gave the captain, she stabbed him in the jugular. Blood sprayed onto the decking. Below the wretched creatures — elfkin, human, and dwarves — shouted, clapped their hands, and shook on the metal grating as he collapsed.

Approaching footsteps. Four sailors raced towards her with clubs and ropes, ready to beat back any slave uprising. They did not expect a Guild War Ender. Alana's saber twirled towards her first opponent, the telchine sailor. She cut towards hir chest, seeking the earthen heart. She found her mark. The telchine crumbled back to the clay from which sie was formed. Alana always found the sort of clean, yet ostentatious death throe of the telchine, gnomes, giants, and dwarves particularly satisfying.

A rope slashed across her forearm, ripping the weave away. Ignoring the pain, she drew her offhand dagger and rotated towards the next sailor, a human. Her first cut was smooth as it sliced the flesh of his arm, the second hit an artery, spraying more blood on the deck and his earthen colleagues.

Roark appeared from the shadows, the head of the purser held high. He threw it to the surviving sailors who stepped back from the sight.

Alana did not pity them. Her two blades struck their flesh; the sailors fell quickly. Blood and earth spread across the decks.

Grabbing the keys off the overseer, she unlatched the first hold.

A young man pushed on the grating from below as she undid the chains. His face was hidden by a long, tangled mane of black hair, but he wore no beard, not even fuzz. He was at the edge of adulthood, his shoulders still slender, but with the promise of muscularity. Though he spent months in chains, he was not faded, his posture was still erect. No doubt bound for the arena.

The slaves made a wild scramble to the weather deck. They reached towards the sky, embracing their freedom as if it were a physical entity. Alana noticed the young man again, searching the crowd. "Ma! Kian!" he called.

She threw the young man the keys to the lower holds. "There are more below!"

He raced down the ladder.

Alana signaled Roark to prepare lifeboats and went below to where weaker slaves were kept. While those bound for the games were kept healthy, less valuable slaves were so emaciated they could barely stand.

Many hung their heads in hopeless dejection; mothers lay unmoving, cradling babes covered in filth. A closer look revealed these children were already dead or dying.

The young man she had given the keys wept over a middle-aged woman's corpse.

"We must move quickly."

"My mother ..." He stared at the corpse with red-rimmed eyes.

Alana took the keys and unlocked the chains. "I'm sorry for your loss, but get those who still hold life. Once safe, we mourn the dead."

Withered women struggled to rise and climb to the upper deck still clutching dead offspring.

The young man didn't move. "I can't leave her here. I can't leave my brother."

"What's your name?" Alana asked.

"Eohan, Son of Aedell."

"Eohan, would Aedell want you to die with her corpse when I abandon this ship to the depths?"

The youth sniffed. "No."

"It would bring your mother honor to know her son saved these other mothers. Get them to the lifeboats."

"Lifeboats." As if the young man came out of a daze, Eohan leapt to his feet and unchained the nearest woman who clasped her dead baby. The woman moaned as he cradled her in his arms and tore out of the hold.

Alana grabbed another woman unable to walk and carried her to Roark who organized the five lifeboats and lowered them one by one into the sea.

She was proud her nephew had the good sense to organize each boat with a mix of healthy survivors and weakened ones. Some slaves dove into the sea and grasped the sides of the boats and other survivors, unwilling to be separated from their families again, clasped each other. Just as well, there wasn't enough room on the lifeboats anyway.

Four more trips to the bowels of the ship, before she and Eohan were able to save all of the survivors. Every bunk, every corner, every chain, Eohan shouted, "Kian, Kian!"

Once the last survivor was out, Alana grabbed his arm before he went below again.

"My brother..."

"We have to go!"

"My brother ... He's a kid!"

"Children were sold in the last port, if you ever want to see him again we must go!"

He glanced toward the hatch.

Alana grabbed an oil lantern off its hook and smashed it across the deck.

"Come on!"

The boy didn't move, but screamed, "Kian!"

Alana almost left Eohan to the flames, but heard Alana Mira! Somewhere deep in her mind, through the smoke, she witnessed an adult version of Eohan tossing a squealing auburn-haired child into the air and catching her.

Damn it. The boy was destined to become a man. A man with a child.

The vision of the child turned to face her. The resemblance to Roark was unmistakable, but she saw something else deep within the blue eyes. Something wild and violent. She was unsure if her vision was literal or figurative representations, but somehow Eohan was bound to the future of House Eyreid. *Damn me to the lowest Realm!*

"Ki--!" Eohan choked as smoke filled his lungs.

Flames rolled closer to them, eating the decking.

Alana rammed her left index and middle finger

into a pressure point deep within the boy's shoulder and gripped his ear with her right hand. "Move."

Forcing him forward, she raced to the last lifeboat. He coughed as she pushed him aboard. He collapsed onto a woman cradling a dead child.

Alana leapt in and lowered the final lifeboat into the water as flames danced above them. Sparks and burning debris splashed down. A spark landed on her arm, but the weave was fire resistant; the bare arms of the survivors weren't as fortunate. She threw out a guide rope to the healthy survivors treading water. Gathering each remaining person, she called, "Help each other."

Aching oldness skulked around her shoulders.

A large wave splashed over the side of the small craft. Beside her, Eohan wept in his hands. The women with babes in arms were too weak to row. The branded girl was trembling under the blanket, now in complete shock.

"Eohan, row," she ordered.

The boy choked on his weeping.

"Row! Or we all die." She shoved the oars into his hands.

Tears streaming down his face, the boy grasped the oars.

"When the ship sinks, it might pull us under. These people are too weak to fight the current. Row."

Though deep in grief and shock, Eohan rowed. Alana was glad to have his strength although his rhythm was off. The boat fell back each time a large wave washed over them. One of the men, a dwarf by his long beard, sank below in the black water. "Get him!"

No one dared let go of the side of the boat or the guide rope.

Without thinking, Alana dove into the icy salt water. She could barely see in the dim, but her strong strokes caught up to the dwarf quickly. She grabbed on his beard, then his arm. When she surfaced, she pushed him half into the lifeboat. *What in the lowest Realm am I doing?* He wasn't even a Fairsinge.

Another wave splashed over them.

She pulled herself in. Roark and the other boats drifted farther away.

She knew the folly, but removed the weave from her face and hair and used the length to tie the survivors to the side of the lifeboat.

"Row," she ordered Eohan. "Row as if your life depends upon it, because it does."

Eohan leaned back as he rowed with more strength than before and found a natural rhythm.

"You're a Martlet?" the woman behind Alana asked. Her voice full of reverence.

Alana didn't answer. She was a Martlet, of course, but she was on Guild assignment.

The word Martlet spread to the lips of the elfkin in the water.

The dwarf asked, "What in the lowest Realm is a Martlet? Looks like a regular elf to me."

Slowly, their boat drew nearer to the shore. Slaves of other species dispersed as they hit the beach, but the elfkin surrounded Roark who turned the boats over in the sand and carefully covered his footprints. Disregarding the survivors clutching to his legs, he strolled northward.

The men holding onto the boat begin to push it as they were able to touch the sea floor with their feet. Alana jumped in the water and helped push until the boat's hull was beached.

The freed Fairsinge sank to their knees and grabbed hold of her legs and hands. "We thought the Martlets were but a myth, Lady." They repeated. "You saved us all, even those of us not of elfkin."

In awe, the words "Martlet" or "Wandering Nobility" were repeated numerous times.

Knowing she might have signed a Guild death warrant, she said, "The wandering Fairsinge nobility are no myth. I heard our people's cry. Speak of me not, lest they come for me. I ride for our people until the water of resurrection washes me clean."

"What house are you from?"

Alana wasn't that stupid. She collected the length of weave and passed around the coin she had taken from the Captain's berth and the ration she kept on her belt. "This is all I can do. Help those too weak to help themselves. To the south is a free port with a strong merchant's union. Find safe passage."

Though soaked through and trembling in the night air, the healthier men and women helped the wounded mothers and branded girl to their feet. The girl pulled away from the man who assisted her and fell to the ground, hiding her face with her arms.

An emaciated woman dug a hole in the sand. She placed her infant within and gently ran the sand over the body. She kissed her hand and pressed it upon the ground leaving a deep print. She created a twisting floral wreath in the sand: the wisewoman's mark.

Tears in her eyes, the wisewoman called, "Goodman, let me assist her." She gathered the trembling girl and the wet wool blanket in her arms.

Alana grasped the wisewoman's arm. "Lead them to Eryedeir Province. Until you arrive there, speak of me not; I broke this Realm's law helping you."

"Eryedeir, yes milady," the wisewoman whispered. She led the girl into the forest. Others followed.

Alana held Eohan's arm. "Go if you wish. You seem kind, and the branded girl needs kindness if she is to survive and find safer shores. However, my nephew needs a companion his own age. Come with us. I will protect and teach you."

She released him.

"What of my brother?"

"How old was he?"

"Ten."

"Children that age were sold in Port Denwort. If we can discover his fate, we will. Make your choice; the fire may bring a patrol. I don't mean to die tonight."

Alana left the boy to his decision and hurried to catch Roark. As she assumed he would, Eohan followed, his bare feet sliding through the sand, his arms hanging limply at his sides.

"Who in the sard is that?" Roark handed her the tarred bag filled with the purser's right hand.

"Swearing is common," Alana reminded him. "Eohan may have what the Guild needs. Just in case Corwin is more upset than I believe he will be."

"We wouldn't need a 'just in case' if you followed Guild law," Roark removed the weave from his face to ensure she saw his scowl.

"If the Guild would help to change these foul laws, I would not have to break them."

"The Guild does not set the law for all intelligent life."

"I never was as wise as I was when I was sixteen." Alana lightly hugged her nephew about the shoulders as they walked.

"You're soaking wet." He studied her arm. "And you should bandage that."

"I fear my reactions are slowing."

"Don't say such things. You were fighting multiple opponents," Roark said.

"Who were common sailors — I feel the creep of age in my muscles, my bones."

"You're in your prime," Roark said. Images of crucified bodies surfaced in his mind. "You shouldn't have let them see your face. And rescuing a dwarf? What were you thinking?"

"I work for the Guild, but I wander as my heart leads," she instructed. "As will you." Not wanting to scold, she changed the subject. "I hope this companion serves."

Roark glanced over his shoulder. "Seems like a bit of a saddlegoose."

"Perhaps so, but I could teach him to saddle a horse."

"I don't think he enjoys the company of men. Or at least I don't sense any chemistry between us."

"Not everyone in the world needs to love you in that way. You might know friendship."

"I don't care about friendship," Roark said.

"How would you know if you have never had any?" Seeing her nephew's stricken face, she added gently, "Besides me. Friends your own age? A peer."

"I ... I have Talia and Jaci. They are my friends."

"They are your friends and mine. But, you must befriend Fairsinge too. I sense something important ... for your future."

"You're sensing something?" He pressed his finger between his eyebrows.

"Yes."

"What?"

"I didn't get a complete picture, only a loose vision through the smoke of the man he is to become," she said. A statement both true and false.

"You never tell me anything," Roark said.

"Only what's important. The rest you must learn for yourself."

Roark raised his eyes to the heavens and shook his head. "We still shouldn't have broken the law. I mean if other species sell their criminals to the slavers or write slavery into their moral codes, it is not for us to..."

"That boy is a Fairsinge. There were at least sixty of our people on that ship."

"But you didn't just save sixty. You saved them all. And you were always going to do it, even before you saw the Fairsinge," he said without compassion.

Roark would have never chosen this path if he wasn't the third born — not that he wished to rule or join the priesthood either. Her nephew's true reason for existing was still an enigma.

They climbed the limestone cliff to the grove where their cache was hidden and horses grazed. A few lazy seabirds squawked on their approach but didn't bother taking flight. The apprentice removed his weave and dressed in riding gear. He saddled the horses as he ought. The master spread an unguent upon the wound on her forearm, then bandaged it carefully, before changing out of the weave and into her riding gear.

Eohan wheezed as he emerged from the brush. He left a trail even a cumberworld could see.

"Are you injured?" Alana asked as she laced a dry undertunic.

"No, milady," he panted, resting his hands on his knees.

"Can you ride?" Alana pulled out an old cloak from her saddlebag and threw it towards him.

"No, milady," Eohan replied eying the horses warily. "I mean I never have, milady."

"Tonight you'll learn."

Alana's dappled gray mare, Talia, stamped her foot and stepped back.

"You can ride Jaci with me. She's more confident with strangers." Roark removed a bar of soap from his saddlebag and threw it at the other boy. "But wash first, if you please, you smell like that ship, and I don't want lice."

"Yes, milord." Eohan inclined his head.

"Enunciate your words," Alana said. "By tradition, the Guild is beyond rank, but the members are still people and people judge."

*

THE YOUNG LORD'S POISE DEMONSTRATED his expertise with the horse, but Eohan felt as if he would tumble to the ground with every footfall. Trying to find his balance, he shifted, causing the cloak the lady offered him to scrunch under his body and tighten around his neck. He pulled it free and was forced to adjust again. A pinprick of heat localized in his legs and spread down to his feet and up his back by the time they arrived in a town with an open gate.

The roads were wide enough for large carts, so the horses trotted through with ease. People bowed their heads and stepped back. Merchants lowered their gaze at Alana while calling if she was interested in medals, fresh strawberries or sausages. His noble escort ignored them all, so Eohan did also though his stomach growled with hunger and quivered with nausea at the fragrance of spiced meat and rotting fruit. The roads were lit with gas lamps and the light from many windows. All around him, elfkin with ears that flowed into a single point rather than three moved about freely. Other than Alana and Roark, he saw no other Fairsinge. *These were all Daosith!*

"Must you hold on so tight? It's rather a warm evening." Roark shrugged backward.

Finally, they stopped in front of a stable.

Eohan's knees wobbled as he slid off the beast. Alana dropped her voice as she spoke to the stableman in Daosithian. He didn't understand the language, but she paid for the horses to be kept.

Roark patted his black horse and kissed its cheek. "Goodnight, Jaci." Then he patted and kissed Alana's gray. "Goodnight, Talia."

Collecting their saddlebags, Alana and Roark walked to a nearby inn. Eohan limped behind them. His groin, thighs, calves, hips, even his stomach ached.

More coin changed hands along with fast-paced Daosithian.

"Only potatoes, Auntie?" Roark asked once they settled next to the crackling fire in a snug corner of the dining hall.

"I fear what more might do to his stomach."

Still unsure of his fortune, Eohan watched the two closely. Alana hummed as she cleaned and sharpened her weaponry. Roark sat beside the fire reading aloud by lantern light, his voice clear and golden. The maid brought three bowls of small red potatoes, a pat of melting butter on top.

After dinner, Alana said goodnight to them both. She squeezed Roark's hand and offered the instruction: "Be kind. He has lost much."

She did not touch Eohan or offer affection, only the directive: "Listen to Roark. Our beds are marked with the sign of the Martlet. No one would claim them if they see my mark, no need to hurry."

His aunt departed; Roark continued to read, now silently. Not knowing what to say, Eohan stared at his feet. His toenails were darkened and bruised. His arms were discolored with welts. His back and shoulders bore scars from the overseer's lash.

Only when the maid approached did Roark speak again, but not to him.

"Another round, please."

Roark tipped the maid for nearly the price of a cup and returned to his scrolls. Eventually, he yawned and went upstairs without a word. Not knowing what else to do, Eohan followed him to the open attic filled with beds, cots, and hammocks strung between the wooden support poles.

An oddly shaped bird enclosed by a diamond was scribbled in chalk on three beds farthest from the stairwell. Lady Alana slept in one. The other two were empty.

"Take that bed," Roark whispered. "I'd rather be closer to my aunt in a setting such as this." He rubbed a thick wax on his face, arms, and through his hair. "Lanoline is good for the skin and protects us from any insects that might have found their way in these beds."

Eohan accepted a squeeze of lanolin and applied it as Roark did.

He lay listening to the snores of other guests, most in shared sleeping arrangements. After so many nights in the dank hold, he wanted to enjoy the space and cotton ticking, but he couldn't. He had never slept alone. His heartbeat quickened. His body became clammy with sweat. His heart twisted with confounded insanity. Ma died on the slave ship. He didn't know what happened to Pa. Kian was in Port Denwort, but only the Goddess knew where that was.

Denwort sounded like a human name, but sometimes dwarvish names sounded human. Moreover, if he left now, what would happen to him in this strange land of Daouail? He didn't know the language. At least with Lady Alana, he had a future. A future with money by the look of it. But could he trust her? Or Roark?

Pa used to tell stories about the wandering nobles. These stories, while full of gallantry and heroism, often indicated the downfall of the proud and mercurial nobleborn or those commoners who stepped out of the sphere which they were born. He shuddered at the thought of being forced to dance on coals until he collapsed or be put in a barrel of knives and rolled down a hill.

A woman's laughter was heard from a bed somewhere in the attic. Mocking his indecision.

From the next bed, Roark whispered, "If you go, I wouldn't be surprised if you're captured by slavers in a day. If you need companionship to quiet your mind tonight, I'll loan you money."

"Companionship? What will Lady Alana say?"

"She'd say use a lambshead, and wash afterward."

Eohan was aghast. He had always been told the nobility, though at times unpredictable, was beyond such base pursuits. "She's a great lady!"

Roark leaned against the headboard. "Who has wandered for five decades. If you take a maid or whore in anger or treat them with contempt, she would undoubtedly dismiss you. Otherwise, remaining in good health and not producing children you can't maintain is all she cares about. She takes men all the time, as do I."

Eohan felt sick. "Together?"

"That'd be peculiar," Roark said. "She conceals her affairs from me, but I'm not ignorant."

"But..." Eohan didn't want to admit he kissed a girl a few times, he had never been with a woman. He had only heard the word lambshead in passing. They were too expensive to be used by butcher's son when lamb intestines could be filled with ground meat and sold as sausages.

As if Roark had read his mind, he said, "My aunt will say, 'Lambheads are an expense, but less expensive than a sick apprentice and much less than maintaining a child.' And she's right."

Eohan processed this bit of information. "Does she have children?"

"A late daughter who fell protecting our House from invaders."

"Many relations must be a blessing," Eohan said. "I hope your sorrow doesn't make it a curse."

"My cousin was a great warrior, but we all have our parts to play," Roark said. "My first-born sister trains to be Doyenne like our mother. My elder brother went to the priesthood as proper for the second born. As the third, I am a wanderer. My younger brother has already secured a noble marriage to strengthen another great house in a few years."

Sounds of laughing and sex grew louder. Memories of the slave ship surfaced. Eohan's back grew slick with sweat. Roark slipped into the bed beside him.

Eohan flinched away.

"I'm sorry about what happened. It must've been awful. That's stupid, obviously, it's awful, but I don't know what else to say." For all his breeding and education about everything from battle to lambsheads, Roark looked embarrassed as he patted Eohan's hand. "Tell me about your life before all this ..."

"Ma always hoped Kian and I would own a butchery together." He sniffed and wiped his eyes. "My pa is a baker. Kian looked like him. I looked more like the smith who fathered me. Sometimes I wished I had looked like Pa. Each night, Pa came by with day-old bread crumbs for stuffing the sausages and honey cakes for us." Eohan's voice cracked. He wiped tears from his cheeks. *What the sard am I doing? A month ago, I was a butcher. Hours ago, I was a slave?*

Roark found a handkerchief.

"Why are you being nice to me, my lord?"

"I'm nobleborn, but I haven't earned my station yet. You can call me Roark," he said. "Lady Alana saw a vision of us as grown men. It seems strange I know, but I trust her visions. She said we become great friends."

"So this is fated?"

"I don't know, but many in this Realm and the next won't be so kind. I've traveled far with my aunt and seen how people treat their apprentices. It doesn't matter the station or race, some people are vile. Alana never raises a hand against me, even when I vex her. She always takes care to not to leave bruises or cuts in weapon's training."

"You're from her own family. I'm a butcher's son."

"Perhaps so, but all her former apprentices speak well of her — and they weren't all nobleborn. Will you believe me if I say she'll treat you at least as well as she treats Talia and Jaci?"

Eohan nodded, though he remained unconvinced.

"She always makes sure the horses are well-rested, clean, and fed, and often uses sweet words and benevolence to ensure their obedience. Besides, you're alone in Daouail. What else would you do?"

"It's true the nobleborn read minds as well as tell the future?"

"I needn't read your mind to see what you're thinking," Roark said.

※

Elizabeth Guizzetti

Chapter 2
A Possible Reality

ALANA TOOK TO HER BED EARLY TO determine if she could see more of her vision. She imagined the man and child within the smoke and drifted into a reverie. She stepped into a dark forest near a slow-moving river and could see the light from a crackling campfire. Three horses, including Jaci, grazed nearby. Talia wasn't among them. Alana felt a sudden ache in her chest. *It only means I am elsewhere.* Yet her heart whispered, *At this moment in this future, I am dead.*

She drifted towards the campfire until she came to a line of chalk and salted earth: a circle of protection.

Beyond it, wearing a stained nightshirt and clutching a wooden doll and a dull-looking dagger, the auburn-haired child, who looked no more than five summers, paced between the three men — Roark, Eohan and an unknown man — who encircled the fire, speaking excitedly to each other.

Dear Goddess, does House Eyreid still stand? If so, why wasn't the child raised within the safe walls of House Eyreid until she was of apprentice age?

The men did not notice Alana, but the girl looked directly at her. She grasped Roark's arm and pointed.

Roark glanced over his shoulder. He had grown into a fine-looking man. His figure was trim and complexion bright, his auburn hair trimmed short, just long enough that it curled a bit. Battles had not scarred any exposed skin. Even the scowl he wore did not diminish his beauty. "I don't see anyone."

"Why don't you see?" The child dropped her doll and stepped in a perfect second guard stance, pointing her dagger out and upwards. Even though they kept her weapon dulled, she already had received some weapon's training. "Someone's there! It's my ghost! Will she get in?"

"Alana Mira, if you can't play quietly, go to bed!" Roark pointed at the bedroll on the other side of where he sat.

Stamping her foot, the girl cried.

Alana's heart sank, but she watched the unknown man stop scribbling in his journal and stare with deadly fury toward the child. "It's Lady Alana?"

He was smaller, more wiry built and commonplace-looking than either Roark or Eohan, but he did share a few features with the massive warrior: hazel eyes, the shape of their brows and cheekbone height. *Was this the lost brother?* "Lady Alana is here?"

The child didn't answer.

Roark pulled the child in front of him a bit too roughly for Alana's taste. "Kian asked you a question." *Yes, it is.*

"She's here somewhere. So are they..."

"Where?" He scanned the wood.

"Beyond the circle. She watches us. I remember this." The girl stamped her feet in rapid succession.

"Open the circle and let her in," Roark ordered.

The child's voice grew shrill. "But I don't want the

shells to get in! Don't make me. I see them!"

Alana had no idea what she was referring to. Nothing of immediate danger seemed to be in the wood. Perhaps the child was born with active mental abilities, that might explain why she was wandering at a tender age. Too young to parse her visions into actionable data, she was no doubt a certain amount of trouble for her guardians — as Alana had once been. Roark's quiescent mental gifts lurked below his analytical mind, but his training gave him, at least, a semblance of understanding. He took a deep breath, and hiding annoyance said, "Calm yourself, or it's your bedtime."

The girl's shoulders trembled, but she clamped her mouth shut.

Eohan held out his muscled arm. "Mouskin, sit with me awhile. Leave your father be." He, too, had grown impressively. His granite jawline and broad shoulders spoke of strength and gave him rugged understated handsomeness. His black hair was clipped short as common in Guild War Enders.

The child glanced at Roark, Eohan, and Kian, and back to Roark.

"Go."

Alana Mira the Second scooped up her doll, scabbarded her small dagger, ran towards Eohan's outstretched arms, and cuddled upon his lap. "You'll help keep guard?"

"We will keep guard." He wrapped her in his jacket.

"Cordelia, Eohan's helping us keep guard," the girl repeated to her doll.

"You need to sit quietly and let us work," Eohan said.

"Sit quietly and let us work," the girl repeated.

Roark stared coldly into the wood. Eventually, he turned, shook out a woolen blanket and set it over Eohan and Alana Mira the Second.

"Kian, if you please..."

"We don't have any," Kian replied.

"I didn't finish my sentence," Roark said.

"Doesn't matter. We'll need to find a town tomorrow or cook some of the horse's oats for Mira. Can we get back to this? I noticed that the digestive tract of the shells..."

Alana smiled. She did not know what "shells" were being referred to but felt relieved. This was just a failed job or an escape gone awry. No one was injured, and the horses looked healthy. They had food for the horses, and while the adults might go hungry for a day or two, the men would ensure the child would be fed.

Alana Mira the Second's eyes drooped, Eohan passed her to Roark who placed her on the bedroll. Frustration gone, Roark tucked her under the blankets with her doll and dagger. She mumbled, but he ran his fingers through her hair before covering her head.

"Tomorrow, we'll have even more problems settling Mira if we don't find someplace warmer," Eohan said.

Roark opened his mouth, but Kian raised his hand. "Don't quarrel; you'll just wake her again. Now, in your observations, did you feel they gained strength in their state or did we witness primitive instinct?"

"I believe we were witnessing a primitive survival instinct. Attack or Eat," Roark said.

Alana perceived the molecules crashing behind her spirit. The future was written. She broke her reverie and allowed her body to drift off to sleep, happy in the knowledge a child, who looked so much like her nephew, would bear her name.

✳

Chapter 3
Village of Taenhel in the
Realm of Daouail

"AUNT ALANA SAYS WE MUST HAVE porridge for breakfast," Roark said as he shook Eohan awake. "Don't want to upset your tummy."

Eohan rubbed his eyes and looked over at the other, now empty bed. "Where is she?"

"Buying you a horse."

"But..."

"Jaci can't be expected to carry two men for days on end. Come on, let's eat. I received a gull this morning."

Roark thought Eohan might be impressed, but instead, his eyebrows raised in a look of utter confusion.

"A gull? A horse?"

Not bothering to answer, Roark sighed, traversed the room of cots, went downstairs, and signaled the maid. Roark might not have Alana's gifts, but he foresaw until they reached the Guild house, cheap, bland food was in his future.

No matter what Alana had said, having another apprentice around would be worse than going home. His mother ruled their holdings and trained the firstborn to follow her. She never had time for Roark (or any of her younger children), but Alana treated him as if he were special. Now she would treat this common sausagemaker's son the same. She was buying a horse simply upon the evidence of a rather idiotic vision. Eohan was worse than an infant lost in the Realms.

The maid set down two large bowls of oat porridge with a few blueberries and a dab of butter on top. Roark paid with the coin Alana gave him and thanked her.

Eohan stumbled in, trying to hide his rags with Alana's cloak.

"In truth? A horse? How will I ever pay her back?"

"You work as every apprentice does. She'll pay for your lodgings, food, and some comforts. The Guild is no different in that respect. As I said, I received a gull. We must move faster than we did last night."

"What if I fall off?"

"You'll die, and we'll sell the horse in the next town or use it as a pack horse or eat it. I bet it'd taste better than sarding porridge." He shoved his spoon into the bowl and took a bite. The blueberries were rather nice, but he tired of bland food for his bland companion. Realizing his words, he met Eohan's eyes. "Don't tell my aunt I swore. She doesn't like it."

"I won't swear in front of her either," Eohan said.

Roark wanted to tell Eohan it didn't matter if he swore since he was a commoner, but decided against it. He didn't know his aunt's wishes on the matter. Though he didn't care if Eohan was dismissed, Alana would know if he caused trouble for the other apprentice. You couldn't put anything past a mind reader.

❄

LISTENING TO THE DIRECTION, EOHAN FIRST feared the difficulty of preparing the blankets and saddling Cloudy, a chestnut mare with a bald face and full white stockings and patch of white on her rump. He feared her flat teeth might bite him if he pulled a strap too hard or pinched her skin. Or her large hooves might stomp his bare feet.

However, once he adjusted the straps correctly, he realized mounting the horse was even more challenging. "She's so tall," he said to the stableman.

"This mare will serve your needs for decades. As I told milady, Cloudy is gentle in the saddle, but daring enough for life on the road." The stableman laced his fingers and gave Eohan a leg-up with a solid push.

From the saddle, the ground seemed far away. As instructed, Eohan pressed her with his calves. She didn't move.

Roark clucked his tongue. Jaci immediately trotted down the street. His high step careful not to step in mud. With a bit of prodding, Cloudy followed.

Eohan clutched the reins as they rode slowly out of town. He wished commoners would stop inclining their heads so close to Cloudy's massive stride — though he had grown up doing the same thing. Alana drew Talia behind Cloudy.

Out of town, the pace quickened. Though he occasionally pulled back on the reins, Eohan got the distinct feeling Cloudy ignored him as she trotted in step with Jaci or turned her head to look back at Talia.

"Don't slouch," Alana said. "Shoulders should be even and straight. Lift from the sternum. Open space in your ribs."

Eohan tried not to be frustrated at the directions which came in a non-stop torrent.

"You're overarching your lower back. Relax the reins. Let Cloudy take a sip of water as you pass the creek; she can get thirsty."

Every adjustment meant another. He had always been proud of his strong physique, but now every muscle seemed clumsy and wrong.

The road was wide, and a gentle grade for walking, but Cloudy galloped up the hill and down the other side at Jaci's pace. Green brush spun beside the clay road. Icy mud flicked on his bare feet and legs. Cold air cut through the old cloak and dug into his skin.

Finally, Alana called for a stop.

Eohan had never been so glad to touch the ground. His knees quivered, muscles ached. He wanted to collapse.

"We've only been riding an hour," his master said, her voice firm.

"Yes, my lady," He straightened his posture.

"Unsaddle all three horses. You will saddle them for practice after we rest."

"Yes, my lady."

As the horses grazed, Alana brought out a scratched leather-bound parchment journal and a wax tablet. She tried to hand the book to him. "Read from this aloud."

He hesitated to touch it.

"I need to see how much you know." Alana signaled her nephew.

"I shall set snares," Roark said before he left.

Eohan gingerly opened the journal. The swirling scrawls were gibberish, though the maps and drawn images were beautiful. "I don't know this."

"Did your mother write out her recipes?" Alana asked, her voice kind.

"She knew them."

"What about market lists? Or if she needed something from one of your fathers?"

The word "fathers" pierced his heart a tiny bit.

"With pictures — but, my lady, Smith never named me."

"I hope I did not open a wound?" Her eyes seemed like she cared.

Eohan thought about Roark's words from the previous night and shrugged. "I feel more angry than sad. I don't know what happened to either of them. I called Foll Baker my Pa — even though he was only Kian's real Pa. I didn't see either of them on the ship ..." An unbidden sob came from his throat.

"Then the smith was a fool and Foll Baker worthy of your grief, as is your fine mother. Show me one of your mother's lists." Alana took the journal and handed him a wax tablet and stylus.

Eohan drew out a list, but his line drawings didn't compare to the crisp ink work he had observed in her journal.

Beside each picture he had drawn, she wrote each word: Pig/Pork, Bread, Basil, Thyme.

They went over the steps to make a sausage. Using these directions, Alana taught him how to create sentences.

Grind pork shoulder three times.
Grind in pork belly during third mix.
Mix in bread and herbs.
Stuff casings

Too soon, Roark returned with a scrawny rabbit — already field dressed — and a few wild parsnips. He started a low fire and stewed the meat and parsnips in a small iron pot without any instruction from his aunt.

After lunch, under Alana's guidance, Eohan saddled all three horses. He noted how Roark went behind him and rechecked the horse's straps. It bothered Eohan that Roark was younger than he but much more capable in the world.

Another ride. This one faster than before. Eohan's

inner thighs began to burn, then chafe. Soreness moved up his spine and into his shoulders. His stomach muscles spasmed.

Eohan feared falling beneath the galloping hooves, but the writing lesson had widened the hole in his heart for his family, especially his little brother. He missed the knowledge of his place in the world. Though he wanted to trust his strange companions' outward affability, the wild coldness behind their icy blue eyes frightened him.

※

L ISTENING TO HIS AUNT'S TORRENT OF instruction, Roark wondered if he had been as clumsy and naive as Eohan when he began his training. He doubted the other apprentice had any idea the scope of their work. Would Eohan go back to sausage making, once he discovered it? It would be nice to prove the Great War Ender Lady Alana wrong, just once.

As they grew nearer to the village of Taenhel, Roark forced Jaci to slow to Cloudy's pace.

"The hamlet's main industry is leather. They sell in the county seat on market day," Roark said. "The villagers have no money to pay a constable full time, so they offered a small stipend for one assassin-in-training."

"You're killing someone?"

"Four someones."

Eohan's mouth hung open.

"Maybe five someones or six, who knows?" Roark said, feeling a bit wicked, but enjoying the shock on Eohan's face.

"This is Roark's first solo multiple kill," Alana said. Her feelings of pride of his deeds enclosed his heart like a soft blanket.

A mile outside of the village, Roark rechecked

his directions. He left the main road, dismounted, and followed a trail to a hunter's shack. Alana said nothing, but the approval on her face spoke for her.

An elderly hunter met them at the door. "The Guild scroll said you would arrive an hour before dusk and here you are."

"We are Guild, yes, but we ride to protect those who can't protect themselves," Roark said with a bow. "This is my master, the War Ender, and this is Eohan, her other apprentice. I am Roark, your assassin this night."

"I made a venison pottage and warmed mead, milords, milady. I hope it pleases you," the hunter said.

"Indeed, it shall, thank you," Alana said. "Roark, would you prefer to sup now or after?"

"After. I'm too excited to eat."

Roark removed his traveling clothing, dressed in the weave, ensuring every inch of his ivory skin and auburn curls were covered. He painted coal under his eyes and the bridge of his nose and carefully adjusted his scabbards. His saber on his right hip, his dagger on his left. Two knives on his left thigh. On his right, a small ration of hardtack, a needle and thread, and coin.

Alana did not recheck his gear this night. She said nothing, except to direct Eohan. "Don't speak until I tell you. Move as quietly as possible."

They left the horses to graze in a quiet glen next to the shack before making their way to a small hamlet of blood and urine-infused masonry buildings. Alana hid in the shadow of a pear tree near the center of town. Eohan sat on the ground beside her and leaned his back against the trunk. Roark crept toward the wooden racks covered in drying deer skins. Above darkened streets, windows were still alight.

He perched on top of a salting shed until his marks approached. Roark scanned the emotions wafting over the village. Their need for vengeance. *They want to watch*, he thought.

He did not want to be afraid. He knew if he faltered in the slightest, Alana would step in. Her patience was legendary, but the warm pride she felt earlier would be washed away with disappointment. She wouldn't show it, but he would feel it.

As the dossier claimed, four sweaty, unwashed Daosith entered the village from the forest. Careful not to step in the light from the windows, they slid towards the large racks of animal skins drying on the wooden racks.

Be quick. Don't tire. Don't let them surround me. Roark repeated Alana's many lessons in his mind.

When the four men were in position, Roark leapt from the shed with his saber in his right hand, the dagger in his left. He stabbed the neck of the closest highwayman who was pulling on a mostly dried deer skin. Clutching on the spurting wound, the man fell forward in pain.

The other men spun around, yelling in confusion.

Roark made a simple thrust into the second man's chest, careful to turn his blade when he felt a rib. Roark withdrew his sword and stabbed the first highwayman again. This time a killing blow. His blade sliced through the third man's flesh in his arm. The fourth turned in time to back away from his swing and arm himself.

The fourth parried and stabbed wildly. Roark disarmed him on the first strike. The fourth turned to run. Roark stabbed him in the back, hitting the kidney. Then struck a final time.

The man with the wounded arm dashed away. Roark raced after him. He quickly paced his mark and dove, tackling him. The momentum knocked them both into a wall of a hut. Straw fell from the roof.

Roark grunted in pain. Dazed, he swung his saber towards the other man. The man screamed as the apprentice felt the give of flesh. He shook his head to clear it as he scrambled to his feet. Maybe it wasn't as clean or quiet as Alana could do it, but he vanquished four opponents on his own.

Roark pocketed four cheaply-made knives and a few coins from the bodies.

"Congratulations, Apprentice. Now finish the job." Alana gestured to Eohan who followed her out of the shadows. "You can see the implications and importance of our employment. Do you still wish to be trained in the ways of the Guild?"

"I'll learn to fight like Roark?" Eohan asked.

"You will learn to fight with multiple weapons, read, ride. This life is as bloody as the arenas, but you're more likely to survive it. You might decide you like assassinations, war ending, or gathering information and writing dossiers. There are a variety of opportunities for advancement."

"Though I hardly made enough to make this job worth it," Roark sulked as he cut off the first man's head with his saber. He kicked the body before he hopped over it and decapitated the next.

"Pay Eohan to do the dirty work," Alana suggested. "He needs those knives more than you."

"Dirty work?" Eohan asked.

"The dossier said to tar and stake the heads as a warning." Roark tossed a head towards Eohan's feet.

The other apprentice paled as the bloody mass bounced towards him. Roark thought Eohan would turn and run. Instead, he gathered the head by the hair.

"Where's the tar?" Eohan asked, his voice still low.

With the realization he wouldn't get his hands sticky, Roark liked another apprentice's presence quite a bit.

*

ALANA COPIED THE LEDGER PAGE INTO HER journal using her three-step code. Listening to the forest's night sounds and the boys and horses sleeping, she was glad she always listened to her foresight, even if the gift only uncovered snippets of truth.

Other than tears for his family and general fear, Eohan spoke nary a complaint. A personality trait that would complement Roark — who often protested even though he was the son of a Doyenne with a comfortable allowance. Now if she could only keep the boy alive until he was trained.

Though the adventures of life kept her slender, her frame softened and sagged in new ways as the sun drew fresh lines on her face. The creep of age occupied her bones more than she admitted, even to her nephew.

If Corwin knew, both boys would be in danger. She needed to progress Roark to the rank of Assassin of the Realms and show Eohan's worth to the Guild before her sword arm slowed further.

✳

Chapter 4
The Muirchlaimhte

EOHAN KNEW THE HORSE WASN'T LISTENING to him. Though he pulled on the reins so Cloudy would slow, the horse continued to follow Alana's lead, galloping wildly down the dirt road. He held on tightly, trying to ignore the constant pain. Eohan lost the concept of time as the forest slurred into an unending green and brown blur until he was blinded by a blue sea.

The horses cantered through the sandy tideline northwards until they reached a beach village with a long dock. At the end of the dock was a large Expanse-faring ship.

Eohan held back the dark memories of the slave hold which crept up his throat as he examined the boat from bow to aft. The forecastle, ending in a large bowsprit, was covered with gun boxes, and Muirchlaimhte was written in gold leaf on the port side. Its rounded-off iron-clad wooden hull held three decks leading to a large aftcastle.

A stately woman in a long coat, directed the sailors and longshore packers surrounding her. He glanced at her ears half hidden by her long black plaits, rather than three points like Fairsinge ears, her ears flowed into a single point. A Daosith. *Gods don't let her be a slaver...*

"She is our transportation." Alana dismounted Talia. "Nyauail!" The women embraced and kissed each other's cheeks.

Once the women parted, the captain shouted over her shoulder. "Nalla!" Without taking a breath, she said some strange words of welcome to Roark.

Roark bowed his head in greeting and replied with his golden mannerisms. Eohan knew he had been introduced once he heard his name. He bowed. When he raised his head, he saw the most beautiful Daosith girl running towards them. Her black plaits bounced over her long blue coat. Her mahogany face was set in a bright smile. Her skin's only flaw was the scar across her left cheek; it made her all the more beautiful. He tried to cover his rags with Alana's too small cloak.

Alana embraced the girl.

"You're staring." Roark elbowed Eohan in the ribs as he stepped forward to take Nalla's hands.

Eohan's shoulder muscles tensed. He knew he shouldn't feel jealous by Roark and Nalla's familiar embrace; Roark didn't even like girls.

"Nalla, this is Eohan," Roark said in the language of the Daosith. Or at least that's what Eohan assumed Roark said in context. Eohan wished he had Roark's eloquence and gift for language. He didn't even know how to say hello in Daosith. He bowed his head but didn't let go of the cloak hiding his rags.

After the greetings, Nalla clicked her tongue at the horses and led them aboard to the lower deck of the ship. Another sailor escorted them up the gangplank

and down a small flight of sternward stairs into the large
Guild cabin. A built-in table and benches were to the
stern below the windows. The port wall was lined with
built-in sea chests and bunks covered in comfortable
looking ticking. The bow held another door. Inside was
a chamber pot.

Outside, there was a bustle of activity until three
sharp whistles pierced the air.

Minutes later, darkness enveloped the ship.

Muirchlaimhte dove through a luminous halo. It
glided across liquid light which danced in every color.
Eohan found no words to express the splendor. Pink
and yellow clouds slipped across the sky; the Expanse
sparkled. Far in the distance, the soft outline of a distant
shore hid in the vapor.

A wrinkled peg-legged Daosith woman carried a
tray of apples, oranges, grapes, yellow cheese, and crusty
bread, which she set on a larger tray that unfolded from
the hull. "Your horses are being washed and inspected
for good health, my lady."

She hobbled out, moments later returning with a
large tub. Nalla and a young man each carried buckets of
water but didn't tarry.

Above, the captain shouted something; sailors
echoed the command through the ship. Eohan looked
out the porthole at the swirling colors as the Daosith
steward helped Alana undress.

"Another new injury?" the old woman asked. "You
must be more careful, Lady; your body is a temple."

"But, Lillia, who would you fuss over if I wasn't
wounded?"

Eohan saw Alana's reflection step into the hot
water. For her fretting, the steward chatted brightly with
the lady as she scrubbed her with an astringent-smelling
soap from head to toe.

Once clean, Lillia helped her out and bandaged

her arm. She rubbed cream into the lady's flesh, dressed her in clean clothes, oiled and braided her wet hair.

"I'll call for more hot water, Apprentice Roark."

The old steward rang a bell. Two more sailors brought in more buckets. Lillia took as much care with Roark's appearance as she had with Alana's.

Eohan hated he did not understand the rotation of the Realms and the binding forces within the Expanse that allowed ships to move from one world to the next having nothing to do with the hours one lived. He heard of such things, but could barely believe he was experiencing them. In the slave ship, he saw no colors, no light, no stars, only the interior of the hold.

The ship sailed upon an ocean of stars. Ahead was a yellow sun with two little white ones spinning around it. "Fairhdel? When will we be there?"

"Not for another three hours or so. Apprentice Eohan, time for your bath," Lillia said as more buckets appeared.

He didn't tell either the steward or his master he had never taken a hot bath before. At home, they bathed in a cool creek outside their village. On the slave ship, the sailors threw buckets of salt water upon them.

The deck shifted under Eohan's feet as the ship sped faster among the lights. Lillia helped him undress. "I'm not..."

"You are an apprentice of the Guild, even if you are all out in the Expanse." The old Daosith continued to unlace his ripped tunic. "I'm paid to serve the Guild."

Eohan found the caress of the warm soapy water agreeable. Lillia's callused hands reminded him of his mother's gentle touch. His heart cracked for his loss, but he forced himself not to cry in front of the old steward, his new master, or other apprentice.

He sank lower in the tub when Nalla entered with a scroll in hand. His cheeks felt hot with embarrassment.

"A sturdy boy like you shouldn't be so shy." The old Daosith ran soap up his arm.

Eohan wished he could sink into the water.

"Captain must speak to you, Lady War Ender." Nalla handed Alana a large, sealed scroll and left without looking towards him.

Once groomed and dressed in a Guild traveling tunic — simpler than Roark's, but sewn just as fine — Eohan followed Lillia to the main deck. When they boarded, the deck was open, but now panes of glass enclosed the ship as if it were a glass honeycomb similar to the slave ship. The thought made him sick, but the crew moved around him without resentment. Captain Nyauail shouted orders, but then the orders were repeated in a shout. Sweat-stained tunics exposed the difficulty of the work, but the crew seemed content.

Lillia winked and pointed to Nalla's back who sat upon the deck with three other young sailors patching a sail.

Eohan approached her. "Hello, how are you doing?"

In a bubbly voice, Nalla pointed out an imminent weather system that would affect both the tidal liquid and air currents of the next Realm. "It might get a little rocky. I hope you don't get Expanse sick."

"I'll be alright."

She looked him up and down. "You look smart in Guild black and green. Why do you journey with Lady Alana?"

"She saved me..." Eohan dragged his sweating palms down his tunic front. He could not think of exactly what to say to her or the other crew members who watched them.

"She saves numerous people; they don't all follow her."

"I need money, so I can save my brother one day.

He's enslaved. My ma...she's gone. My pa was...lost."

"Oh, I'm sorry." Nalla's callused hand squeezed his. Her dark eyes filled with sorrow. Her lovely face was so expressive.

Hoping to see her smile again but unable to think of anything clever, he asked, "What's it like to work on the Expanse?"

❋

IN THE AFT CORNER OF THE CAPTAIN'S MESS, Alana sat so close to Nyauail that her leg brushed against the captain's. The threadbare cushions covering the hard cedar benches only added to her discomfort.

"That boy..." Nyauail hissed.

"Should I have left him there on the beach?" Alana whispered back, keeping her voice low so as not to be heard by the crew. Not wishing to offend her friend, she refused to do a habitual scan for nearby assets or weapons. A friend was one of the best assets a person could have anyway. "Roark needs a friend, I've foreseen it."

"Just be more careful," Nyauail whispered. "Daouail made an official complaint to the Guild. Everyone is talking about it. And I can't say I agree with burning a ship — any ship."

"I already killed the crew. Who's everyone?"

"Kajsa and Doriel --which means Seweryn must know about it too."

"Hardly everyone. We're ending a war together next month. As long as I keep Seweryn in employment, he's loyal."

"Don't wave this off. Corwin has crucified those who flaunt guild law. As he enters his dotage, he has become more zealous about making the Guild respectable again."

"How so?" Cloaking her fear with movement, Alana stood, paced the deck, sat on the sea chest across the room, stood and sat again.

"Seweryn was saying Corwin wants every noble Fairsinge and Daosith family to send their third born out into the Realms and join the Guild — not just the small Great houses who can ill afford to have their Martlet's idle. He will not welcome a commoner to the ranks."

Alana did not doubt these words. Corwin had come to detest the Guild traditions toward commoners. "Even if every third-born entered the Greater Realms, they won't all join the Guild. We will never be respectable. Besides, to end wars, we need to be hated and feared. Common blood works just as well as noble blood for that."

"You're preaching to the converted."

Doubt of her quick reflexes and mental abilities washed over Alana. "Am I among friends?"

"Don't be stupid." Nyauail crossed her arms and leaned back against the inner hull.

"Then I have a favor ... for Eohan. If in your travels, you hear of a slave boy sold in Denwort...."

"Do you know how many slaves are sold in Denwort?"

"A boy of ten. With strawberry blonde hair, but hazel eyes like his brother. His given name is Kian, son of Aedell the Sausagemaker." She removed the ledger page from her pouch. "He's one of twelve who were sold."

Nyauail sighed. "Give me that before you're caught with evidence of your crime. I do not promise anything."

Alana passed the piece of the ledger which Nyauail hid in her coat.

"I have a daughter to think about, you know."

"If you find him, I'll do everything by the law," Alana promised but regretted her words. She shouldn't have to respect laws so despicable.

✳

Chapter 5
Guild House of Olentir
in the Realm of Fairhdel

ROARK FOLLOWED HIS AUNT IN THE LAND OF painted hills and three suns — though, from this angle, he could only see the largest one with any clarity. The other two were blurry pinpricks of light orbiting the first.

From the docks, no intelligent life was visible, only hillsides covered in tiny pink flowers and a herd of long-haired black deer. The stag lifted his head to look at the Fairsinge who approached by foot. His antlers gleamed gold in the morning sun. Two fawns frolicked under their mothers' watchful eyes, but otherwise, the herd consumed the new grasses and flowers, ignoring them.

"Why aren't the dubfeid running away?" Eohan asked.

"They're wild but protected by the Guild. They are used to small groups of people on the hillsides," Alana said. "As long as we walk at an even pace and keep our weapons sheathed, they take no heed, still, be mindful of the fawns."

45

Seeing the unasked questions on Eohan's face, Roark said, "Their bleat can be heard for miles, so they make a good alarm. And the Guild harvesters collect the hair from their winter coats for the weave."

Alana led the way around three curving knolls to a keep built into a rocky hillside of amber-colored granite. The unbroken spires of the keep appeared smoothly carved rock, however within tiny unseen holes, the guard watched for approaching violence. The stone's warmth radiated towards Roark, as they passed through the first gate. It felt good to be home. The home where he could be himself, not House Eyreid where he must follow the rules of court.

The party was welcomed by the guards as they walked past a large cloister built out of the same tawny granite. Roark told Eohan, "Every guild house supports a community of lay people: shepherds, cooks, brewers, weavers, and the like." He pointed out storerooms, commissary, latrine and other important locations.

Four large stone-carved hooded beings held an archway. Alana cupped her hand slightly in front of her chest and made a sweeping gesture before a hooded figure who saluted in kind and opened a door.

Every footstep seemed muffled, though they trod upon stone pavers. They walked down a long, red hallway with black doors and stained-glass windows at the end of it. The bright lights danced.

Alana knocked upon a door. They entered a windowless cell where the only light originated from a hole in the ceiling that illuminated a solid wooden table in the middle of the room.

A tall bearded Fairsinge in white linen emerged out of the darkness. His pale, deep wrinkles revealed centuries of sneering.

"House Master Corwin," Alana bent her head at the slightest of inclines.

Roark knelt. He was glad Eohan followed his example.

Alana moved towards the table. She opened the tarred sacks to show him the dismembered right hands. "Proof as requested for the job at sea. I am pleased to announce Apprentice Roark completed the Taenhel job alone."

Corwin replied with an indistinct sound.

"We bring the Guild its tribute, Master Corwin." Alana set a box of jewels upon the table. Roark rose and offered two knives collected off the highwaymen at Taenhel.

Corwin's flabby wrists were thin with age, but it did not stop the quickness by which his long, manicured fingers measured each jewel, coin and blade which he recorded on a long, thin parchment. Roark felt the house master's eyes upon Eohan.

"And the boy?" he asked.

"Is my newest apprentice," his aunt said with ice in her voice.

Corwin's piercing black eyes did not leave the other boy. "Is he anything else? One of the slaves from that ship?"

"What ship?"

"The one you set aflame," Corwin said.

"A lamp spilled. There is a reason every sailor fears fire," Alana said.

Corwin remained focused on the boy. "Is he to be bound?"

Roark felt his spine tighten. Eohan had no station or relatives to protect him.

During his own binding five years prior, Corwin called his mother a whore. Furious, Roark had shouted at him, "My mother is a Doyenne." Corwin had slapped him twice for speaking out of turn. Alana stopped the third blow with the promise to cut off Corwin's hands if he touched Roark again.

Corwin had let him go, but his next words sent chills down Roark's spine. "I do what I will to apprentices. Any apprentice. Even yours."

Alana had laughed but without joy. "I'd hate to see our Great Houses fall into chaos because of a difference of opinion between two Martlets. Or is your vow to your House of no importance to you?" she had said.

Corwin never touched Roark again. Roark was overcome by the need to defend Eohan, but he remained quiet and allowed his master to protect her apprentices.

"Eohan's not yet to be bound," Alana said.

"And if he is lost?"

"Then we wasted no time binding an apprentice. I want two young men for my honor guard. This one has an impressiveness to him, don't you think?"

Finishing the count, Corwin's sneer disappeared; a frightening smile spread across his face. He held out a large waxed envelope to Alana. "Are you taking him to your bed?"

"What I do with men is not your concern," she replied.

"You're lucky you're useful to us, Alana, but someday you will weaken," he muttered still clutching the envelope. "Your team awaits in room seven."

"Thank you, Lord Corwin."

Corwin dropped the dossier on the floor.

Alana inclined her head and gestured at her apprentices to rise. She kicked the dossier back to Roark, who plucked it from the ground.

Another hallway, another darkened room.

Alana entered first. Both young men followed her closely. As with all strategy rooms of the Guild, the exact measurements were elusive as the walls seemed to withdraw out of reach. If one weren't careful, one might run into a support or a forgotten chair hidden in the darkness. As they moved toward the center, the gloom parted enough to see the outline of a heavy oaken table and six chairs where two Larcian dwarves and a Daosith enjoyed mugs of Guild mead while they waited.

"Lady Alana," the Daosith, Lord Seweryn, said, standing and opening his arms wide. He smelled as if he had not bathed in a month. His silver hair was greasy across his ashy dark skin, black tunic stained with sweat, but Alana still embraced him with the familiarity of an old lover reunited once more.

Alana gestured at the dwarves. "Allow me to introduce War Ender Lady Kajsa Goldsvein and Lord Doriel Angrock." At the Daosith, "Lord Seweryn of House Illysdum, this is Eohan, son of Aedell."

"Weapon?" Kajsa, the dwarf fighter asked. Behind her as always was Doriel Angrock: her brother-in-law and brother-in-arms. They also wore the weave, but their golden hair and full beards were neatly plaited. Roark was glad to see he knew everyone on the team. Kajsa was once Alana's apprentice, and Doriel and Seweryn were trusted colleagues.

"Brain," Alana replied.

Corwin grunted behind them. "Enough pleasantries. The Guild needs you to move if you are to stop a war."

"Roark, Eohan, secure the perimeter," Alana ordered. "I don't want outsiders to hear my plans."

"Why do you fear the truth coming to light, Alana?" Corwin asked.

"Get out," she said.

"I leave because I choose to." He disappeared into the darkness as if he was never there.

Roark took a piece of chalk from his pocket and handed Eohan a small bag of salt. "Trace my steps."

He chalked a protective circle upon the stone floor. Eohan followed with the salt. Roark raised his arms above his head. "I ask the Goddesses and Gods bless this circle. No sound will escape. We will not be seen or heard. Even when we leave this place, our goods will only be touched by those within the circle."

A high-pitched tone engulfed the room, which settled into a low hum. Roark felt the vibration of energy within his bones as the circle manifested.

"That's it?" Eohan asked in a whisper.

"What did you expect?"

"A ball of light?"

"Real magic isn't like how street buskers do it."

"Boys, discuss that later," Alana said in a low tone Roark knew to obey immediately.

He sat in the chair to Alana's left, and Eohan sat on the chair beside him, now quiet. Roark was glad Eohan knew when to obey as well. He didn't want to have to teach him everything.

✳

Chapter 6
The Persidal Valley in
Realm of Larcia

O N HORSEBACK, KAJSA AND DORIEL surveyed the great valley filled with daisies, wild parsley, and carrot that the telchine coveted. Hemmed in by granite mountains, where the dwarves could retreat, this could be a death trap for either side. They studied their maps and Guild dossier for several hours before deciding on the best path for Alana's army to march and sent a crow.

The dwarves rode for the smallest and most remote granite fort in full regalia of Lady Bjalla whose estate was a month's ride to the north. The next fort was several days ride to the north, over hard terrain. Kajsa's heavy velvets signified her the rank of general, Doriel was her man at arms, a cavalry lieutenant.

"Hey Oh! Brothers, we bring word from the rift," Kajsa called from the base of Fort Ebnora.

The gate opened without hesitation.

"One would think they weren't on the edge of war," Kajsa whispered. Doriel grumbled in agreement.

Kajsa leapt from her horse and strode forward,

shouting, "Who is in charge here?"

A one-eyed sergeant on a peg leg wobbled towards her, clumsily bowed. "What's the fuss all about?"

This man suffered more than her dossier had told her. "The telchine army arrives in three days."

"Here? Why would they come here?"

A murmur ran through the crowd.

"They are coming!" Kajsa was careful to mix in the truth; if any authenticators were among the company, she would give no hint of lying. "It is only by chance we are this far south. A trusted friend gave us this information. We need to prepare."

"We lost three men and a lady trying to get here," Doriel added quickly. "We are hungry. Our horses need rest, Sergeant..."

"Blazedigger. Molin Blazedigger." He said, "My ... Our troops may be few, but we train each day." He snapped his fingers. A young fair-haired dwarf hurried over for their horses.

"I hope so," Kajsa said with a practiced touch of sadness in her voice. "They plan to take this fort to gain the foothold in the Realm. Where can we find reinforcements?"

"Fort Moldus is ten days' ride."

"Doriel, send a message to Fort Moldus. Sergeant, I would like to inspect the troops." She turned towards the small company. "We may have to fight to every last one of us. The telchine has hired the Guild."

Groans, coughs, and choked breaths filled the entire fort.

※

Chapter 7
City of Mavpotas
Realm of Si Na

THE ELFKIN RODE MILES PAST THE CITY until they reached a primitive wood hut that looked as if it had been abandoned for a century. Seweryn made a bed for himself in the old hayloft while the others dressed in full regalia.

With her apprentices behind her, Alana crossed a brick bridge covered in black soot. Below was the place between three Realms where the Expanse grew thin. Within the ravine, a person could stroll across from one Realm into the next, which is what gnomes, telchine, and dwarves had been doing. It might have been used for trade and prosperity; instead, someone used it to steal. No one knew which side raided first. Only that mistrust had spread between the dwarves and the telchine.

Inside the telchine city of rising spires, they were greeted with cheers and a shower of rose petals. Their towers and cathedrals in the city looked magnificent, but up close it was disgusting. Tenements surrounded each block of gasworks that provided hot water but belched out noise, smoke, and foul odors. The stone streets were covered with straw to dampen noise, but on close inspection, it was covered in the feces of animals and other rubbish.

"What do you see?" Alana asked Eohan.

The clay, asexual species did not fear disease the way other species did, but Eohan thought that might not be the answer his master sought. And he didn't want Roark to judge him a cumberworld.

"There is no right answer. Tell me what you see," his master said.

"Though the telchine is at war with the dwarves, the populace seems relaxed – just going about their day. I don't sense fear of the coming armies. They are happy we are here because they think it means they will win."

"Very good, Apprentice."

Alana stopped in front of a small candle shop on the edge of town.

Two telchines the color of river clay greeted them by bowing and clasping elbows.

"I'm called Theklas, this is my offspring Elpis," one said.

Theklas's flesh was cracked and weathered, while Elpis's was smooth but other than the signs of age, they looked nearly identical. Their eyes were the same color as the yellow grass, and their hair the color of the mountain soil. Their thick fingers were callused and their arms muscled. Observing them, Eohan discovered they held traits of both genders as well as traits of neither. No wonder they did not have words for "he" or "she" in their language.

Theklas shook hands with Alana. "We will help any way we can, my friends. We open our home to you."

Alana thanked them and turned back to her apprentices. "Go down each lane, find anywhere the edge of this Realm touches another. After speaking with Theklas, I shall meet the Viscount. Meet me in the royal aerie in an hour."

"Yes, Lady Alana," Roark said. Eohan echoed him and followed the other apprentice as they rode down the dirt road.

✻

"HOW WELL DO YOU KNOW THE VISCOUNT Melittas?" Alana asked Theklas as sie led her through the candle shop and up the stairs to their apartment.

"I was a soldier when I was young. I'm just a chandler now."

"And your offspring?"

"I train hir to follow me. We were told if we house you during your stay in Si Na, Elpis will serve the Guild's needs, rather than fight. We have a private stable for your horses."

As Alana expected, her contacts were unimportant to this battle in every way.

"Bring me to Viscount Melittas. I must speak to hir."

Theklas's blinked a few times. Hir voice quivered. "Yes, of course, War Ender, but don't you want to refresh yourself?"

"No."

"Elpis, see to our supper and the care of the War Ender's horse," Theklas ordered in the tone of a suggestion and squeezed Elpis's shoulder before they left.

Alana enjoyed the telchine's tender way with their offspring during a decade-long training period. Unlike the elfkin who birthed their children, the telchine were molded full-grown from clay and given the breath of life from their progenitors. Elpis being left alone with fire and a warhorse must mean sie was between age five and ten years.

55

Theklas led Alana into the most central building within the winding streets. It was even more elaborate than Alana expected, a jaunty red stone mansion under a thin layer of lichen and moss, overlooking the creek.

"I wish to see the Viscount," Alana said to the guards in front of the house.

They looked over at Theklas who shrugged. They sent word to another servant, but as soon as the door was opened, Alana pushed past the guards, assuming a ninety-one percent chance her rank would protect her.

"My Lady, this is highly irregular," a guard said.

"Where is the Viscount's solar?"

Sie paused.

"Don't keep a Guild War Ender waiting."

"This way." The guard brought them to the Viscount in hir expansive solar. The stone tiled floor was obscured in a soft carpet. Depictions of florae and peacocks were frescoed in the thick plaster walls embedded with gold. Maps covered the heavy oak table.

Melittas was everything Alana expected hir to be.

Hir pupils indicated sie was shocked that Alana forced her way in, but like all diplomats, sie held a relaxed coolness. "War Ender, I didn't expect you yet, but welcome."

"We must speak strategy before we handle secondary worries."

"My forces spent the past winter months recruiting in order to strengthen the next phase of military operations," the Viscount said. "I contacted the Guild to help us clear the valley of dwarven troops."

Sie spoke with large hand motions, in the carefully clipped language of the telchine. Hir clay-colored skin was artificially smoothed with greasepaint, and hir hair was dyed the color of fresh grass which matched the embroidered green linens, sie swathed hirself in. Alana could never trust leaders who used the Guild but put commoners in a place to take the blade if everything went wrong.

"The valley on the other side of the Expanse in Larcia?" Alana asked.

"Of course, but it is an ancient ground of the telchine. Just as your own Realm split into Daouail and Fairhdel, Si Na lost Larcia."

Alana nodded noncommittally. "My understanding is your family owns an aerie."

"But gryphons are..."

"Exactly what we need. Do you wish to win or not?"

Alana showed the Viscount her "official" plan. Melittas tried to argue about the ancient ties between the telchines and gnomes, something that she, a wandering elf knight errant, couldn't understand.

Stepping closer to the Viscount, Alana repeated the plan in louder Telchinish.

※

A LANA BOWED AT THE HEAD MARE, ORTZI. Though she didn't bother to rise from her nest, she did bow her feathered head. Her mate, Piltzi followed suit, as did her offspring.

"I mean to end this war, but I need your help, Lady," Alana said.

The mare stared at her with deep golden eyes. In Telchinish broken only by the slight guttural rumble of her feathered throat, Ortiz replied, "Gryphons don't sully our feathers with fighting; that is only something you bipeds do."

"Your Viscount Melittas, myself and two apprentices who will serve as my honor guard need to be carried high above the skirmish for survey, and I shall cast the occasional illusion in order to protect lives."

The mare glanced at her spouse and the two eldest gryphons spoke a few sentences in their own language.

Behind her, the apprentices approached. Roark as confident as always; Eohan full of fear.

A crow flew into the stables and landed on the floor. Alana tossed it a bit of apple and untied the scroll from its foot.

"Kajsa reports: 'As expected the dwarves have hidden in their underground cities; the outskirts and farmland are unguarded. The word of the Guild's involvement has spread to them. The gnomes remain neutral.' Good." She paused. "I'm hungry. Elpis is making us a supper."

Following Alana out of the stables, Eohan asked, "Why is it good that the gnomes remain neutral?"

"Because we don't want to have to fight two armies," Roark said.

✳

IN THEKLAS'S CHAMBERS, EOHAN FOLLOWED Alana as she set out clothing, checked the repair of each weapon, and made ready for the morning. She turned and bumped into him. She pressed her lips together and looked towards the ceiling — an expression he had seen on his mother when he got underfoot — but Alana did not chastise him. She just continued with her list.

Roark sat upon a bench by the window, slowly running a whetstone across his saber. Nerves creased his brow, but he remained in one place. Eohan wished he could be as still as his companion. In honor of their hosts, the two nobleborn spoke in Telchinish for most of the night with Roark repeating in Fairsinger to Eohan. He felt so stupid, so uneducated, so terrified of the clock ticking down 'til morning.

Roark said in their own language: "Be careful, Auntie. I think the Viscount wants to put a dagger in you for asking for the gryphons. Or sie might try to take on Eohan — a commoner on a noble mount."

"A dagger?" Eohan asked, his voice raised as if he spoke a question, ending in a squeak. "And a gryphon?"

"It's like riding a horse," Alana said.

"Only if you fall, you fall farther," Roark said with a terrible grin. "After all it's the gryphon who does most of the work. All you need to do is wear your livery and hang on."

"But if sie comes after me?"

"I suppose you should learn how to deal with it." Alana said, "Clear the room."

Roark jumped into action, pushing the furniture out of the way. Eohan turned to help him.

Without warning, Alana punched Eohan's ribs. He doubled over as he grimaced in pain.

"That's how it will come. Then you'll be dead, so there is no use worrying about it. Now try to hit me."

He curled his fingers into a fist and jabbed toward her chin. She sidestepped out of the way.

A growl tore its way up his throat. He lunged, and she easily backtracked away. Another lunge. Another dodge. Eohan's face grew prickly with heat. He started panting. *How could an old woman move so fast?*

Alana slammed Eohan into the wall. He tried to struggle, but the more he resisted, the tighter her grip on his throat.

"Stop. You will hurt yourself."

Though Eohan felt the rage and despair flutter around his heart, he stopped.

"If you can't learn to control your emotions, you're a danger to us all. Can you do all I ask of you? If not, you better stay in this room and help Elpis care for our horses until the war's over. It's your choice." She released him.

"If you stay here, learn Telchinish so the experience isn't completely wasted on you."

Being parted from his protection and translators seemed more terrible than facing a battle. "Yes."

Theklas didn't say anything, but from the corner of the room, sie drew hir offspring closer.

Turning to them, Alana said something in Telchinish.

Feeling his cheeks flush, he begged, "Don't leave me behind. I can do it. Tell them I'm going with you."

"They know that," Roark said behind him. "She apologized for instructing you in dodging, but you feared Larcian daggers. Help me put this table back. Now she is apologizing for your most recent outburst.

"Theklas is talking about how sie is glad Elpis need not fear Larcian weapons since Alana must teach us so harshly to avoid them. Now they are discussing how disrespectful offspring are to their progenitor's wisdom. Goddess, I need to work on my Telchinish, I can barely keep up with them, but that's the gist."

Eohan wondered if Roark was truthful until Elpis pulled away from Theklas with an eye roll. Sie grabbed a stack of cards from the cupboard and then pointed at Eohan and Roark and the table. Sie flapped hir hands like an open mouth and said, "Progenitors."

That needed no translation.

*

Chapter 8
The Persidal Valley in the Realm of Larcia

A T THE FIRST LIGHT OF DAWN, EOHAN FELT Roark's warmth move away from him in Theklas's comfortable bed. Not wanting to feel Alana's wrath again, he quickly rose and nearly stepped on the telchine family who slept on mats on the floor.

Before dressing, he glanced in a mirror at his ribs and throat. Alana had not left marks.

"It isn't even sore."

"I told you she always measures her blows. She wants to teach you to fight, not hurt you," Roark said from behind him.

Eohan dressed first in linens, a layer of woolen and then an outer layer of rich green velvet edged in black as a Guild Honor Guard. He looked like a respectable gentleman, but somehow Roark wore it better. He wondered what Nalla would think of him in this costume.

"She wouldn't think of it at all," Roark said. "She's a sailor; her main concern is if it's warm. You could report that it is. Especially with the gloves and cap."

"It's sarding annoying when you do that."

Roark eyed Eohan's reflection in the mirror. "At least, I'm not pining over someone I spoke to for ten minutes."

"Boys, you need not wake our hosts," Alana whispered in warning as she applied lanolin to her face. "They were kind enough to leave us cheese and oats. Ensure you break your fast."

"Sorry, Aunt Alana," Roark said sweetly.

She painted her lips and eyelids. "Use lanolin or wind will burn your cheeks and lips, boys."

Though Alana included Roark in the order, Eohan knew she directed him. Roark wouldn't need to be told. He glanced at Alana's face again. Neither smiling with exultation or frowning with anger, she seemed almost passive. He wondered what that meant.

Once they left the chandler's home, Alana took Eohan by the elbow and put him on her left, Roark drew close to her right side as they walked. "The first battle will come today, dear ones. We cannot stop it any more than we could stop a wave in the ocean."

"So fretting comes to naught," Roark recited. "Yet we always do."

✻

THE FRAGRANCE OF CEDAR, HAY AND FLUFFY, freshly-washed feathers enveloped Eohan. Queasiness crept from his chest into icy aches in his joints. "I only have to hold on to Celena's bridle. She'll do the rest." He tightened his grip as the land pulled away from his feet and the strap on his cap pressed against his chin, the wind threatening to rip it away. He closed his eyes as they smashed through a cloud. He opened them as he felt the gryphon level.

As the young mare was taught to do, Celena followed the matron of the family who bore Alana. Examining the sharp beak and claws, muscular wings that pushed wind into his face, he thought, If I see Cloudy again, I'll never fear her. Beside him, Roark rode Celena's sister, Calendra. His expression was too relaxed to be astride a beast who could bite him in half.

Flying ahead of the company on Celena's father, the Viscount Melittas held the telchine's banner aloft. Sie shouted words of freedom and ancient homeland until hir company clamored to their feet, creating a din of sound and motion. Looking at the telchine marching below, he knew some would die, and their leader did not care. Queasiness burned into sadness.

The telchine's clay-colored flesh was protected only by woven blue and green cloth armor, but they moved with the beat of the drummer behind them. They sang to their land of Si Na: The Giver of Life. They begged Hir to remember them even if they should fall in the foreign Realms, their woven green and blue standard waving in the wind.

Eohan felt a tremble deep in his belly as they crossed the Expanse to the Realm of the dwarves. For a moment, the two Realms overlapped. A flash of light blinded him, and a loud pop rang out. The valley was full of yellow daisies hemmed in by primordial forests growing up the side of ancient granite mountains.

The sky was moist and cold, but wind dried out Eohan's eyes. He licked his parched lips and tried to wipe his freezing cheeks on his tunic sleeve.

Black smoke filled the air. Below, the telchine burned a farmhouse. The thatched roof ablaze, a dwarven female ran with two small children in tow, while a few adult farmers tried to protect the farmland. As commanded, the telchine consumed everything in their path with flames. The farmers burned to death, their screams terminated as they crumbled into gravel.

From the east, a small contingent of dwarf soldiers rode towards the burning farms. The telchine army raced towards them, and a hurricane of chaotic violence morphed the field of daisies into a plain of fallen granite and clay. Muscles aching and unable to catch a full breath, Eohan could barely recall how he came to be with this strange pair of Fairsinge Nobility, in this strange Realm, on the back of a gryphon.

Wondering if he could help, Eohan clenched the reins tighter. He almost turned towards the field below.

"Roark!" Alana screamed from above him.

In less than a heartbeat, Roark was beside him holding Celena's reins still and straight. He spoke to the gryphon, "Forgive me, great lady, I feared your rider might lead you astray."

"I follow my mother. Not the War Ender astride her, Nestling."

"Thank you, lady, that's good to know." Roark inclined his head. "If you distract my aunt again, I'll kill you," He hissed at Eohan. "We are here to stop this war."

"Why doesn't she stop it!"

"This is a battle, not the war," Celena said, "My mother said it won't last longer than an hour at most."

"But how many will fall?"

"Hopefully enough to make our client listen to reason," he said sadly. "Do as you're bid. You don't want to see my aunt furious. Or the gryphon's mother."

Though he was inwardly afraid, Eohan muttered, "She's just an old woman."

"She's an old woman who could easily trounce us both with one hand tied behind her back if she wanted. Her experience bests your strength."

"And I will crush your disobedient bones in my beak if you order me out of formation again," Celena said. "I've never tasted Fairsinge. I doubt my mother would be too disappointed if I ate you."

"If you eat him, I want a bite," Calendra added.

Roark laughed, but Eohan wasn't sure the

gryphons were joking.

*

THOUGH HE SPOKE CROSS WORDS, ROARK understood Eohan's sentiments. By their reputation, the chivalrous gryphons also experienced agony at the chaos below. He did not see the battle. Instead, he watched dwarven mothers running with babes in arms and children in tow while a few farmers tried to protect their farmland and cattle. Not only did the farmers fall, but so did at least one woman and her child. Their screams echoed in Roark's heart as the air around them burned. The telchine fires ate everything in their path. Flying above the battle didn't make Roark clean.

As Calendra swooped lower, he saw a face stare upwards before crumbling into granite. An unknown young dwarf reached towards his enemy in the moments of death. As dwarf blood ought to do, it clotted into sparkling crystals. The shards sprayed nearby telchine and dwarves injuring them. He grumbled under his breath, "Why won't Auntie just let me kill hir, then this could be over and done."

He pushed one self-loathing thought deep in the depths of his heart. If the dwarves contacted us first, I would be on the other side killing the innocent telchine and burning their farms.

Alana's plans ended the fighting before the dwarves could bring reinforcements, but battles often bore a filthy chaos that couldn't be contained. Assassinations were so much cleaner. He wished he could tell Alana that. Maybe she would die of old age before he had to tell her that he didn't want to be a Guild War Ender. He had no stomach for the loss of innocents. He didn't want to lose her or disappoint her, but he would do both eventually. Then she would treat him like she treated everyone else.

*

WITH THE LARCIAN DWARVES SLOW TO retaliate, the telchine easily won the first day. The few surviving dwarven soldiers limped west back to their fort as the telchine made camp in the scorched valley.

After the battle, as Alana instructed, Melittas flew above the troops, flying the banner of their homeland until the company was on their feet, cheering.

Roark and Eohan cared for the gryphons and returned to the command tent with only the most basic genialities to Alana due to her by rank. She found them later, lying together fully dressed on a pile of bedding.

She brushed her fingertips across her nephew's brow. His temperature felt normal. She checked Eohan's pulse and temperature. He too seemed healthy.

She sat on her cot. Perhaps she pushed Eohan too hard; Roark was doing his best with an untrained companion. There was little to be done about it; tomorrow would be worse.

A raucous roar sounded outside the tent. Cheerful drunkenness soared through the ranks like a disease. A few telchine made themselves unfit, staggering around, vomiting in corners, pissing on tent flaps.

Though she didn't believe in bodily punishment as a rule and it pained her to do it, Alana didn't have time to think of another option. She ordered Melittas, "Have them flogged."

"Telchine don't make violence upon our comrades," the Viscount replied.

"If you wish us to win this war for you, do as I

command," Alana stared at Melittas until sie turned hir head away. So the telchine didn't flog their own but would sell them into slavery if they were useless or criminal. They would march onto Larcian soil and steal from the dwarves.

"Do what you will, but I will not," Melittas whispered at hir feet.

She snatched a nearby drunken telchine soldier, clapped hir in iron chains, and led hir throughout the camp with the tip of her blade in hir back.

Humiliation sobered the ranks. A few spoke of desertion, but most feared the Fairsinge who invaded their ranks and rode the mount of royalty. The woman was feared most of all. Good.

A gull flew towards her, landed in front of her tent and waddled inside.

She looked at the scroll upon his foot.

It held one word in Nyauail's hand: Found.

Smiling, she tossed it into the camp stove where Roark stirred stew. His bright smile was back, but circles had developed under his blue eyes.

He spoke in the ancient long-dead language of elfkin before their split into the Fairsinge and the Daosith Realms. "Eohan changes his mind as a fly beats his wings. It's exhausting." His hands trembled as he carefully ladled the stew into a bowl and handed it to her. "I don't see how you read so many minds at once."

"Did his emotions overwhelm you?" Alana took a bite of stew, savoring its warmth more than its flavor.

"I could handle it during the battle, but afterward, I was exhausted. I apologize for that. I should have helped you out there, but I ached for sleep, and Eohan ..."

"As long as you can serve the plan, eat and sleep as your needs dictate," she said ignoring the instinct to embrace her nephew and offer him encouragement. Even a boy as caring as Roark would not like to be embarrassed in front of a peer by an aunt in her dotage. "However, I'd like both you boys to spar with covered daggers for one hour this afternoon. Then I'll set a dummy bail for Eohan to practice against."

Roark glanced at his feet as he tried to hide his distaste for Eohan touching the saber bequeathed to him by his mother. He failed. "What weapon?"

Alana removed a steel claymore of dwarven make from under her cot. "I think this suits him. I found it yesterday."

Too heavy in the hand for Roark, the sword looked to be that of a common foot soldier, set with a wheel pommel and an unadorned split guard. Still, the blade was sound, the pommel sturdy.

"Tonight, you and I will practice a few mental skills to help you focus. Both of you will turn in early. Fear makes Eohan stupid, exhaustion more so."

Roark nodded.

"If he lives through this, we must find his brother," Alana said.

"Why? He's just one boy."

"Either Eohan will become a War Ender and make a powerful ally. Or I will claim he died in training, and buy him a sausage shop. By his gratitude, he will be an unknown safehouse. Either way, useful to you."

Roark wiped his hands on his breeches. "Why do you say such things?"

"I won't be around forever."

He looked her in the eye. "I don't want to be a War Ender." *Are you vexed with me?* he asked in his mind.

"You won't have the protection of the highest rank, and assassins don't always have close friends. Make allies now, dearling."

"When Seweryn arrives, I must be agreeable to him," Roark said. "Even though he doesn't always bath regularly."

"Good boy."

"Did you really sleep with him?"

"Do you really want me to answer that?"

"No."

"Good, because my affairs are not your concern."

"Corwin's jealousy grows worse, Aunt."

"Our expertise protects us," she lied and brushed the hair from his brow. She knew why Corwin hated her, but there was nothing to be done about it. Their daughter was dead. "Try not to worry. Just follow the plan."

Yes, tomorrow would be worse. Alana thought, *but the day after the worst of all.*

✳

Chapter 9
Persidal Valley
in the Realm of Larcia

MORNING MIST COVERED THE VALLEY. IT was almost peaceful except for the murmur of hidden fear in the hearts of the marching telchine underneath her. Most of them did not want the valley. Even the ones who would benefit financially didn't want to fight. Good. She could use this to her advantage. The biggest disadvantage was a telchine Viscount who wanted to prove hirself as a great leader, worthy of song and story. Eohan's fear alarmed her. She must take care he did not undermine the mission.

She circled back and signaled Roark and Eohan to come near. Ortzi called out, and the other gryphons flew to her.

"Roark, acquire a drum."

Her nephew returned quickly from the errand.

"Stay with the Viscount," she ordered. "Perfect weather for duplicity."

Alana tapped a direction with her foot to Ortzi and flew towards Fort Ebnora.

Eohan asked, "What does that mean?"

She was too far away to answer. Maybe Roark did. She visualized a battalion of the telchine marching. She pulled that image from her mind. The wind hummed around her. "Shadow Army March. Shadow Army March. Shadow Army March." She pushed the image onto the ground. She played the marching beat upon the drum. Ortzi flew lower.

The mists coalesced. Dark forms rose out of the ground and paraded towards Fort Ebnora. With each drumbeat, the shadows grew more dense and detailed until the illusion matched the image in her mind.

"I can't believe my own eyes," the gryphon called out in Telchinish. "Can all elfkin do such wonders?"

"Any elfkin of the Guild, my friend," Alana lied, then added truthfully, "We protect those we serve. Let the arrows land upon the ground, not our companions."

A volley of arrows filled the sky and landed upon the grassy valley, forming a line. The illusions of telchine soldiers continued their march towards the fort.

Another volley of dwarven arrows fell, and a third. Arrows continued to rain to the ground, but the deception of telchine soldiers did not stop.

✳

FROM THE WALLS, KAJSA GAZED THROUGH the mist toward the marching telchine. Cries of the not-yet-battle tested young were heard throughout the fort as their arrows did nothing against the invaders. She worked with Alana enough to recognize an illusion when she saw one, even still her breath caught in her throat. Their clay-colored flesh and long strands of green hair almost reminded her of grass on the breeze. Though dwarves hearts were strong as the granite from which they came, darkness grew in their spirits. Even her own.

"There are scores of them," Blazedigger whispered.

"And beyond another regiment."

"Yes. Elf magic might protect from arrows, but the invaders will fall from steel to the heart." Kajsa tapped her broadsword and whistled. Her warhorse trotted to her side.

She jumped off the battlement and clambered upon her horse. "Hardy up, fellows!" She shouted, "We fell some telchine yesterday, and we shall bring death upon the invaders today! Larcia is our land!"

Echoing shrieks filled the sky; Kajsa glimpsed upwards. The gryphons carrying Alana's apprentices and the Viscount Melittas approached.

The winged creatures circled the sky as if they were vultures, but Kajsa knew they would not come lower. She pointed towards them. "The Guild ..."

"I don't suffer telchine!" Blazedigger huffed.

"They are not telchine, brother. Look and see."

Kajsa understood why Alana wanted two young men as her honor guard. The sight of three Fairsinge was effective. Where Roark was lovely to behold and a little prone to jesting, the new boy was especially effective at appearing grim. When grown, Eohan would be a sight. If she lived through the day, Kajsa might see if he fancied a dwarf companion. She didn't mind men new as long as they did as they were told.

Death might meet her, Doriel and all within this fort today, but Alana's plan must work, or the telchine would spread across Larcia. Many other Larcians — dwarves, gnomes and animals — might die.

As planned, Doriel blew his trumpet as the real army advanced.

The gate opened.

"For Larcia!" Kajsa charged out the main gate with a shout, her sword ready to break against the first telchine unlucky enough to meet her. With flashing steel and thundering hooves, she attacked. Blazedigger and his soldiers roared behind her.

Dust rose into the air. The air grew foul with the smell of crystallizing blood falling to earth as stone and clay.

＊

THE FLAP OF THE GRYPHON'S WINGS AND the thunderous beat of its giant heart did not obscure the chaotic screams, shouts and screeching metal against metal below. Eohan watched hoping to see the clean plaits of Kajsa or Doriel, but it was only violent confusion. He was glad though he wore the claymore on his back; he was not expected to use it yet on anything other than a bail of hay.

Following Alana, they flew over the fort and saw Kajsa riding her horse and slashing her greatsword on a telchine who crumbled back to the clay. Without looking at her opponent, she rode through the battle. Slashing her weapon to the left, then the right. Her flashing armor and sword grew muddy and dull with each kill.

The dwarven defenders fought hard, ignoring the mud, dirt, clay, crystal.

At the end of the hour, the telchine had not gained the fort but had not retreated either. The dwarves sequestered themselves inside. The telchines made camp upon the battlefield again, however, exhausted from battle and this close to the enemy, there was no carousing to be heard throughout the day and evening.

Deep in the night, Alana and Roark dressed in the weave with care. They left Eohan sleeping in their tent and crept past the sentries. Not one telchine or dwarf witnessed the shadows moving across the battlefield to the base of the fort. Alana set sawdust charges and blasting caps on the hinges of the dwarves' granite walls.

Roark hid in the shadows, where the rising sun would blind anyone who looked his way.

✻

Elizabeth Guizzetti

Chapter 10
Persidal Valley
in the Realm of Larcia

AS THE SUN ROSE ACROSS THE FIELD, ALANA mounted Ortzi who stepped towards the Larcian fort. Ortzi screeched at the fort door, louder and more magnificent than any herald's trumpet. Once the sound died on the wind, Alana called out, "I come to negotiate in good faith."

Blazedigger shouted from the wall, "Never!"

Alana raised her hands.

Roark pushed the ignition switch.

Seconds later, a loud boom echoed through the valley, followed by a thud as the door fell to the ground in front of Ortzi's feet. The gryphon screeched again. This time loud enough to echo across every room of the fort.

"I ask again if you would consider negotiation, with the Guild acting as mediators," Alana said.

"We will never surrender," a young man with a red beard called out. Alana made a note of him as a troublemaker.

"Shut it, boy!" Doriel shouted, "I want to hear the General and Sergeant speak!"

"Children suffer from this continued conflict with the telchine," Kajsa shouted, "We have already lost farmers and their children. We have lost brothers and sisters-in-arms. Yet, if we lose this land, Larcia is lost. How can we negotiate?"

"The Guild only seeks to stop this war and find peace." Alana said, "We seek a fair and profitable compromise."

Older, wiser dwarves began speaking. Every time a word of opposition to a possible treaty filled the air, Doriel shouted it down while Kajsa begged for peace from her people.

✳

THE GRYPHONS WERE HOUSED; THE ARMIES made fires and waited while the leaders spoke with Alana on a wooden pavilion created by the newly collapsed fort door. Roark, long accustomed to seeing the secrets all intelligent beings hide, listened.

When the first knife appeared for Alana, he deflected it and killed the would-be assassin before sie came in blade length near his aunt. The telchine crumbled back into the clay from which sie was born.

Holding piles of fresh clay, he openly begged loud enough that all who stood by could hear: "Allow your honor guard to sit beside you, Lady War Ender. You are in danger!"

The rumor that Alana was in danger spread predictably through the ranks.

Alana met eyes with Melittas. "You hired me. Am I safe in your presence?"

"Yes, War Ender," Melittas replied. Hir voice did not betray the duplicity.

She turned towards Kajsa. "General, am I safe in your presence?"

"Yes, Lady War Ender," the dwarf said without

any hint of warmth in her tone or her eyes.

Beside her, Blazedigger watched Melittas with a new weariness. "My Lady War Ender, if it pleases you, we might offer one of our own in ransom to provide you with even more security."

Melittas quickly also added, "I would also offer one of my own."

"Good, but unneeded." Alana dismissed Roark and Eohan who went back to the grounds.

"That blade ..." Eohan whispered.

"From the Viscount," Roark whispered back. "I've always felt it's the height of bad manners to kill a War Ender whom you hired."

Eohan smiled wanly. "Now what?"

"Now we wait."

In position, they waited. Hours were broken by the occasional game of cards with a curious dwarf or telchine who had never met a Fairsinge. The dwarves were mostly interested that Fairsinge "bled like animals" while the telchine were curious "how they knew they were male."

From the cliffs above the pavilion, Seweryn flashed a mirror towards Roark's face. Leaping to his feet, Roark raced towards the tent screaming, "Watch out! Lady Alana."

As planned, Eohan fell a few paces behind him.

Once Roark was in the correct position, Seweryn, dressed in a realistic looking beard, but a telchine uniform in greens and blues shoved a dwarvish knife into Roark's chest. It missed all the major organs, but Roark still screamed from the pain of the knife piercing his flesh.

Seweryn was gone before anyone could catch him.

Agony rattled in his chest as Alana bellowed, "You tried to kill me, Lady Alana of the Guild, though we negotiate in good faith? For Roark is more than my Guild Honor Guard, he is also of my own nephew. If he falls,

I fear Guild retribution will be swift for both sides. You offered your own people as ransom, should I kill them in cold blood?"

Roark didn't hear the council's answer as Eohan and a nearby dwarf carried him to another tent. In the commotion, they weren't stopped as the dwarves and telchine joined forces in search for Roark's killer.

Eohan gently placed Roark on his cot. He knelt beside Roark pressing his massive hands to his chest. "We need all these people out! Good Sir, bring a medic!" Eohan screamed. The dwarf raced out.

Fighting against the pain, Roark pressed his hands over Eohan's hands, trying to staunch the blood. Looking into the other apprentice's face, he was glad his aunt found a friend for him who wouldn't leave his side.

Seweryn materialized from a dark corner wearing only the weave with a first aid kit. He sprinkled a potion upon the wound and bandaged Roark efficiently. Then extracted a bottle of Daosith wine from his bag, uncapped it with his teeth, and took a swig. He handed it to Roark who downed the rest, forgetting Alana's earlier message about being friends with the assassin.

"Eohan, don't look so glum," Seweryn whispered in Fairsinger. "Both sides share a common fear of Alana's retribution. Common fear is common ground."

Rustling through a bag, Seweryn found a bottle of telchinish whiskey, took two large gulps and handed it to Eohan.

"Dwarves love self-sacrifice for one's comrade in arms and telchine are very loving to their offspring. They might not understand the idea of 'nephew' in our sense of the word, but they understand it's a familial relationship. That's why I stabbed him, not you."

Eohan sniffed and wiped away his unstoppable tears. "Alana told me. I just didn't expect this much blood. Sorry."

Roark wanted to tell Eohan not to be sorry. No one ever cried for him, but the elvish wine made him too sleepy to comfort his friend.

"Take a drink to settle your nerves, but don't get drunk. Clean the bandages every two hours. Keep Roark still and give him a single pill every time you clean the wound. As night falls, call in the servants and explain Roark is near death. Understand?"

"Yes, Lord Seweryn." Eohan choked out.

"Chin up, lads, your part is almost over," Seweryn said before he rolled under Roark's cot where he napped while Alana entered with a telchine doctor.

Staring at the blood-stained bandages, sie muttered, "I can make a mud pack to cover the wound."

"The bandages are better for our kind," Alana said. "Any other suggestions?"

"I've never seen the red blood of elfkin. Does this mean you are related to the humans? I know someone who keeps a human slave..."

"Then leave! I'll care for him," Eohan snapped. Though it wasn't part of the plan, he straightened to his full height and backed the doctor out. Roark had never seen such passionate anger in his companion's eyes.

Alana gave Roark a kiss on his brow before she followed.

Watching his companion's shoulders slouch, Roark asked, "You alright?"

Eohan nodded. Seweryn voice whispered from below Roark's cot. "Calm yourself, Son of Aedell. Roark will be fine and so will you."

Roark moaned about the pain whenever a servant approached the command tent, but otherwise kept to his cot. At midnight, he officially died.

Alana and Eohan burnt a draped effigy filled with feathers in front of all the assembled dwarves and telchine. Eohan stared at the fire, unblinking while Alana keened loudly.

High on granite cliffs, both wearing the weave, Seweryn and Roark watched his funeral. Watching Alana weep, Roark wondered what would happen if he fell in battle. The rest of his family would be glad to be rid of him. *Would Alana truly mourn me? She claimed she was getting older, slower. If she fell, would I keen for her?* Not knowing disturbed him. The agony of never seeing her again disturbed him more.

Roark was pulled from his thoughts when Seweryn whispered, "Everyone's busy. We can safely cross the divide without being seen."

"Agreed. My lord, I must know … Are you the reason Corwin looks for Alana's downfall?"

"The lady's belief that Martlet vows are more sacrosanct than Guild law is why Corwin seeks her fall. You know this."

Seweryn stepped through the Expanse. Moments later when they passed into Si Na, Roark caught up to him.

"But did you?"

"Yes."

Roark kicked a stone. It almost rolled down the hillside, but Seweryn stopped it with his foot. "Please don't cause a fuss. I'd hate for Alana's devotion to you all be for naught." He sidestepped Roark and headed north where he had stayed before.

"How could you? She's old enough…"

"Alana might be your aunt, but to me, she is a woman — and I cherish the memory of our time together."

A rolling heat filled Roark's stomach. "Do you think Eohan…?"

Seweryn flashed a cold smile and shook his head. Not in the negative but in contempt. "Since this seems to matter to you, may I point out that I was never her apprentice. And I was a man of twenty-five, not a youth.

I was shy. She took pity."

"Twenty-five? Really?" Roark was surprised. He figured that most Guild apprentices employed brothels or commoners.

Seweryn shrugged. "Alana teaches you to be in the world. During my apprenticeship, I wasn't allowed to partake in any enjoyments that might distract me. Corwin feared a mistake might blush his reputation and hurt his chances at promotion. One night, Kajsa and Doriel went to a brothel as their habit. I did not partake. Alana asked me. I said yes. We were not in love. She insisted we use lambsheads, so she didn't bear any more children. She needed a distraction. Your cousin's death was on her heart. I hope as clumsy as I was, I offered her some comfort. She offered me a few skills, so I no longer fear I'll make a whore weep."

"That's disgusting."

"You brought it up," Serweyn said. "Your jealousy is surprising."

Alana used half-truths all the time, so Roark decided he could too. "I'm not jealous; I fear Corwin," Roark said.

"Oh is that all? Well, that just proves you aren't stupid, lad. A few nights with a man — especially another Martlet — is not why Corwin growls."

"But those were his words."

"Words hide true emotions as well as they show them. I thought Alana was teaching you to use this." Seweryn flicked Roark's brow. "Use it."

✳

STARING AT THE WITHERED ASH-COATED embers, Alana allowed herself a moment to be taken by the grief of her fallen daughter. Saray had laughed easily and was kind to animals and children.

Much to Corwin's dismay, Saray had no talents for ending a war, but she had been an expert swordswoman. On the day she died, ten fell from her sword and she had stacked their bodies into a gruesome wall to defend the nursery. *If only I had been home to fight beside her, perhaps Saray would still be alive.*

Alana pushed that thought from her head. "I leave you both to your folly. My own blood fell on this worthless field."

She turned to the command tent. Eohan followed.

She had not taken two steps when Blazedigger cried out, "No, don't leave us!"

Melittas agreed. "Please, don't leave us, War Ender. Help us!"

An hour later, the war was over.

The dwarves would not lose their land, but Viscount Melittas could send trade envoys freely paying only one silver coin in duty per every ten pounds of earthen goods and linens if sie traded anywhere in the valley. Dwarven merchants paid the same rate for all metal goods and ales. The duty for gnomish spider silk would be a single copper per bolt, and since gnomes didn't leave their hollows often, their merchants, who were from all beings, could travel freely from Si Na and Larcia. This would profit the telchine, the dwarves and the gnomes.

*

Chapter 11
Outside Mavpotas in
Realm of Si Na

"I'M NOT SURE IF I AM INTELLIGENT ENOUGH for The Guild, my lady," Eohan said as they rode away from the telchine city towards the port village. Though he felt the horse's cantering movements, after riding gryphons, Cloudy seemed to be part of him. Out of training and instinct, he leaned forward as the horse jumped a hedgerow and shifted his weight as the horse landed.

As did Alana on Talia, and Jaci, who was acting as a packhorse, since Roark was 'dead.'

"It's so much. You saw to the end of it even before we started."

"That's why you train."

"And you didn't make someone dance on coals for their misdeeds," Eohan said softly.

Alana chuckled. "The old stories don't quite capture the work, do they?"

"They are strangely more exciting ... and less somehow," Eohan said. "But what of my brother? I can't leave him to his fate."

"Kian has never been far from my mind. We must remain cautious, but I asked contacts to look into Port Denwort. We head to Dynion as soon as we pay the others and check in with Corwin."

"We wanted to open a sausage shop." As the words left his mouth, they felt bitter on Eohan's tongue. He didn't want that life anymore when a life of adventure awaited.

"Is that still what you wish?" Alana asked.

Thinking of his little brother's safety, Eohan lied to himself, "Yes."

"You're sure you would rather be a butcher than work for the Guild?"

"Yes." *And I will believe it ...*

Alana plucked a small burlap sack of coins from her saddlebag and threw it at him.

"That will fund your ride to Fairhdel. Keep the clothes; you can sell them to help finance your brother's freedom."

The bag of coins was more than he ever held before, yet she had several times more in her saddlebag. His pulse quickened as he wondered if there was some way he could have it all.

Faster than he could see, she grabbed Cloudy's reins. Eohan felt panic as the three horses were crowded together. Jaci, riderless, neighed uncomfortably from behind him.

Without warning, Alana's dagger was at his throat. He leaned away from the blade. A squeeze on his neck, then piercing pain between his ribs. Falling. He landed flat on his back on the dirt road. Alana rode away with Cloudy and Jaci behind her.

The wind had been knocked out of him, but as he rose, he discovered no injuries. He checked his belt, his knives were still in place, but the scabbard on his back was empty; she had taken his claymore!

"I'm sorry," he shouted after her. "I'm sorry."

He walked until darkness fell. A pinch began in his heels and rose to his shins. His fingers grew numb in the cold. He hid them in his sleeves.

Something rustled through the bushes beside him.

He screamed as a huge animal appeared from the brush. A stag pawed the ground, but Eohan focused on the sharp-looking, six-tined antlers.

He receded slowly, putting space between him and the beast.

He leaned against the tree. Wet moss was cold on the back of his head.

A lump grew in his throat. He cried for the loss of everything. Kian, his mother, his new life and friends: Alana, Roark, Kajsa, Doriel, and Nalla. He would never see Nalla again.

His tears stopped when he heard laughter and voices.

"Lady Alana?"

No answer. Eohan feared he was being watched. As he was taught, he shifted his weight to the balls of his feet and started scanning the underbrush for threats.

Four telchine approached on the road, singing in drunken song. They stopped when they saw him.

"What have we here?" The closest one wearing a frizzy yellow beard said. "Are you a dwarf?"

"No, I'm Fairsinge."

"A what?"

"An elfkin."

"Really?" Another answered, his voice slurred with alcohol. "You look like a dwarf to me."

Eohan backed away. Struggling with his limited Telchinish, he said, "I just helped save your people from the dwarves. I flew beside the Viscount!"

"You a friend to the Viscount? Sie buy you that

fancy tunic? My own offspring go around half-naked thanks to the damn taxes for hir war."

Another laughed drunkenly. "Maybe we should take this dwarf's shirt."

"Maybe this dwarf should give us all he got."

"Leave me alone." Eohan drew a knife from his boot. He slashed wildly in the air toward the one with the frizzy beard. He did not connect. His knife cleaved the air again.

Fists and open hands knocked him to the ground. Eohan slashed upwards with his knife. One grabbed his arm and smacked his hand. He dropped the knife.

Laughing, the telchine pulled at his tunic. Eohan kicked upward and hit hir in the groin. The telchine grunted from the impact, but sie was not affected as Eohan assumed sie would be.

Eohan scrambled to his feet. One telchine hit the back of his legs. He fell forward into the mud. Laughter filled his ears.

✳

LEAVING CLOUDY AND JACI TO GRAZE, ALANA rode Talia towards the men surrounding her apprentice. They didn't look as if they were robbers, just drunk villagers celebrating the feast where the bard's exclaimed the Viscount defeated the dwarves with guile. Even though the telchine had been the first aggressors, it would be some time before these people learned to trust the dwarves — or any outsiders — again.

Drawing her short blade, Alana slapped the first telchine using the flat, followed by a wide arc to hit the next opponent, knocking hir to the ground. She kicked the third in the face. Liquid clay spurted across her boots.

The fourth grabbed Talia. Alana sliced hir across the face. It was not a mortal wound, but it might scar.

Three ran off, leaving the final telchine bleeding clay into the dirt, holding hir broken nose.

"Get up, Eohan."

The boy peeked at her, his face swollen where one of the drunks hit him.

"Finished with your tantrum?"

"Yes, my lady. Where did you come from?"

"Will you ever lie to me again?"

"No, my lady."

"Will you ever let greed overpower your senses again?" she asked.

"No, my lady."

"Good. Cloudy is a hundred paces north." Alana said, ensuring her voice left no room for discussion. "You dropped your things."

Eohan grabbed the small bag of spilled gold coin and discarded knife from the ground.

"I was never far out of earshot. Come along."

Trotting after her horse, he said, "I'm sorry."

Cloudy and Jaci looked up from their grazing at her approach. Cloudy seemed happy to see Eohan and trotted to him. Jaci neighed again. She put her hand out to the gelding and petted his nose as Roark would have done.

Once Eohan was upon his horse, she scolded, "I needed to demonstrate the price of greed before you acted upon any inclination."

"You knew?"

"If you plotted against me or any member of the Guild, my answer would be your death. If you acted upon it, you would face crucifixion. Understand?"

"Yes, my lady."

"You lied to a mind reader. Why?"

"My brother ... I don't know."

"Truth now. Do you wish to be released from this life? I will take you to Fairhdel. We can find a village and open your shop with the payment I gave you. I will seek your brother, and if he lives, I'll bring him to you."

"No, my lady." The boy wiped tears from his face. "I want this life."

"When we arrive in Olentir, you will be bound to me as my apprentice."

"Yes, my lady." He stared at his riding saddle, trying to stop the flow of tears. His voice cracked. "Will you tell Roark?"

"I don't see why every detail of your education concerns my nephew, any more than every detail of his education concerns you."

"Are you saying..."

"I am saying, though Roark has never let greed overtake his good sense, both of you have disappointed me. I swear apprentices will be the death of me."

✳

Chapter 12
The Muirchlaimhte

A T THE EGRESS OF THE GUILD CABIN, EOHAN watched Nalla run a line of rope through a honeycomb window, raising a sail. The crew moved in practiced sequence by order of the deck boss. It was a dance that Eohan didn't understand. The air was dense with sweat and condensation in the enclosed deck. Outside the hexagonal windows, a mass of multiple colors of the Expanse swirled in the mists. A streak of red flashed by, followed by violet. The chaos reminded him of battle. Feeling dizzy, he reached for a nearby barrel lashed to the deck.

A callused, withered hand was on his arm.

"You fine, Guild Apprentice?" the deck boss asked him.

"Yes, Sir. I just wanted to..." He paused.

"I ain't got all day. Spit it out, boy."

"Nalla ..."

"Wash the idea from your head. See a whore once we land."

Eohan raised his hands. "I just want to talk to her."

"How old are you?" The deck boss punctuated his question with a shake.

"Ei-Eighteen."

The man made a noncommittal grunt and a few syllables in what might be the Daosith language. Digging his narrow fingers into the muscles of Eohan's bicep, he strode across the deck to where Nalla wrapped lengths of rope in tight figure-eights.

"This boy wants to talk to you. You want to talk to him? Don't take all day."

Eohan wanted to share everything. His mouth was dry. Thoughts jumbled his brain, each word pushing towards his mouth. Struggling for coherence, he couldn't speak.

Nalla saved him. "Did you like your first job?" she asked.

"It wasn't what I expected." He pushed his sweaty hands into his tunic pockets.

"I don't suppose it ever would be. My mother has some stories about her apprenticeship; she preferred transport and was lucky to procure a ship."

"So many people died ... on the battlefield."

"More were saved."

"You sound like Alana."

Her eyes twinkled. "No one of the Guild is all that different."

"How did you get that scar? Battle?"

"Shore leave. A drunk threw a bottle — not at me, but it hit my head," she said.

"It makes your face look even more beautiful, kind of dangerous." Eohan held back a shiver as he remembered the drunks which attacked him.

"Men," she huffed, but she still smiled. His heart beat faster. He had to let her know.

"I love you."

Nalla's rhythmic coiling halted. She dropped three

loops which she quickly gathered. "You barely know me."

"The first day I saw you. You're the most beautiful woman ... every time I see you my heart might burst. I didn't see you when we boarded and thought I might sink into the sea."

"I was just running an errand for my mother." Her smile grew wider.

The deck boss whistled. Nalla finished coiling ropes and tied them off.

"Is there another?" Eohan asked.

"Another?"

"Another man?"

"No," She laughed lightly. "Or not yet anyway."

The deck boss made two short whistles.

"Do you like me at all?"

"You're fetching and sweet so I'd like to know you better, but I love this ship and sailing the Expanse. I want to be deck boss someday." Nalla's bronzed cheeks blushed darker as her eyes left his face and looked past him. "I'm not to be on the road you walk upon."

Eohan glanced over his shoulder. Nyauail wore a deep frown causing her brow to wrinkle. He spun around and inclined his head. "Captain Nyauail?"

"If you wish to learn the sailor's craft, you may stay aboard," Nyauail said firmly. "However, you've no claim on my daughter's heart — or time." She handed him a scroll. "Give this to your master."

Nalla met his eyes once more and gave him a small smile. It didn't matter she didn't love him. He would love her forever. Even if she didn't love him back, the compassion in her eyes, the directness of her speech deserved adoration.

Flush searing his cheeks, Eohan crossed the deck. The eyes of entire crew were upon him. He hurried below and handed the scroll to Alana. Unable to look at his master, he stared at her boots. "I'm sorry if I caused you embarrassment."

She laid a hand on his shoulder. "What a desolate universe it should be if young people feared to speak to one another."

"Nalla said she didn't know me."

"That girl always had a good head on her shoulders. Perhaps you two could take a short walk once we finish the binding." Alana broke the wax seal on the scroll. "This will bring you some happiness, I should think."

"What is it?"

"More information about the man who bought Kian."

"Nalla's mother ... gave me that ... but she was vexed with me."

"I doubt that very much. Nyauail is our friend." Alana patted his shoulder. "You're overwrought. Rest. Call the steward to bring you another bath or a massage. I shall read this and plan."

"Do you think we really found him?"

"I hope so, but it doesn't change the fact we must go to Olentir first. Rest."

✻

Guild House of Olentir in the Realm of Fairhdel

Eohan knelt onto the dark stone floor. The House Master's long uncut nails, sharp and thick as knives, scratched his skin as the old man put a hand to his throat.

"You wish to apprentice with the Guild, boy?" Corwin's bloodshot yellowed eyes focused upon Eohan,

"Yes, House Master Corwin. I wish to be a War Ender."

Corwin threw back his hand and slapped Eohan across the face, the tips of his fingernails scratching his cheek. "The hedgeborn will not be a War Ender in my lifetime!"

"He has a highly analytical mind," Alana said. "And I have foreseen it."

Corwin slapped Eohan again, this time on the ear. It took his entire will not to fight back as instructed.

"Have you bedded him yet?" Corwin sneered at her. "I should kill him."

Out of the darkness, Seweryn, Kajsa, Doriel, and Roark appeared above Eohan.

The Daosith and the dwarves stepped over Eohan, putting themselves between the House Master and him.

Roark helped him to his feet.

"Master, if I hadn't heard it with my own ears, I would never have guessed jealousy makes you stupid," Seweryn said, his eyes laughing.

"I'd rather work with a shrewd hedgeborn than a stupid noble," Kajsa said, "Now bind him to Lady Alana. I stand here as a witness to the truth of his character."

Eohan couldn't believe they were defending him. If they only knew about the forest, they would not defend him!

Corwin looked down at Eohan again, and if he hadn't just been hitting him, he asked, "What is our code?"

Trying to remember each word that Alana taught him, he recited, "We champion the side we are paid to champion or the side which brings the Guild the most stability as a Realm is a form of payment."

"And?"

"I must never disregard a bird without giving a reasonable written excuse, nor will I love anyone more than my oaths to the Guild."

"Come."

Corwin led the party to a door carved with two crows intertwined with leaves and scrollwork. Eohan opened the door for him, half expecting a blow, but Corwin just went through the door, swishing his linen robes against the floor. Eohan realized how strange it was that Corwin no longer walked in silence as the others did.

Feathers, straw, and bird guano covered the floor in the large brick room. Each wall was littered with large hollows of missing brick which housed the Guild's messengers: crows, gulls, and pigeons.

Corwin opened one gate.

Six birds hopped out of their holes. Corwin grasped Eohan's arm. With a bladed ring, Corwin sliced open the flesh on his wrist. Pressing the wound to his mouth, the housemaster sucked until blood pooled on the skin.

The birds lifted their heads and picked at the droplets of blood. Jiggling his foot on the floor, Eohan tried to ignore the pinpricks of pain as their beaks plunged into the wound. He forcibly tried to relax his arm, but his shoulders and neck tensed. He locked his knees and grew dizzy.

"Bind yourself to your Master," Corwin said.

Light-headed, Eohan pressed his finger into his wound and pressed a bloody thumbprint into Alana's forehead.

In the moment of binding, other marks materialized upon Alana's brow: one was Roark's, one was from her own fallen daughter, and one sparkled with dwarfblood. Not just any dwarf, but Kajsa. He could envision the other four, but they were just young faces of people he didn't know.

He looked to Corwin. Several bloody thumbprints spotted his brow: Fairsinge, Daosith, dwarf, telchine, and human. He recognized two: Seweryn and Doriel.

"For the faith you put in me, I teach you in the ways of the Guild as your abilities dictate," Alana said.

He would remember this day in the years to come. However, he didn't quite understand the meaning of her words in the moment.

"Bind yourself to your messengers."

Trying to make sense of it, Eohan pressed his thumb into the open wounds and called to the first crow. He pressed his bloody thumbprint into the back of the bird's neck, so she and future generations of her nestlings could always find him.

As his future spread out before him, he understood the gravity of his vow. He was bound to Alana until he earned his rank and he was bound to the Guild until he fell in battle or died from other causes.

He fainted.

✻

LANA KNELT AND FELT EOHAN'S CAROTID artery. "A little weak, but getting stronger."

Corwin nudged the boy with his foot as the marked birds pecked at his open wound, finishing the binding ceremony. "I told you he was too fragile to be a War Ender."

Alana was about to answer, when Seweryn interrupted brightly, "Would you prefer he vomit on your shoes as I did, Master?" The man laughed, but the words dripped with venom.

Roark and Alana lifted Eohan by the shoulders. Doriel and Kajsa each took a leg. The four carried him to an empty sleeping cell.

Depositing him on the bed, Roark grunted, "Auntie, can your next apprentice be a gnome? They are much lighter."

No one laughed, though Kajsa half smiled.

Corwin followed them; his linen robes swished against the stone floor.

"How do you propose to teach him, Alana?"

"Our first stop is in Dynion."

"Why is that?"

"There is always violence among the human city-states and brigands in the wilds."

Corwin narrowed his eyes before he disappeared silently into the darkness.

"Thank you, my friends, for protecting my apprentice," Alana checked Eohan's pulse on his neck as Roark bandaged his arm.

"It's highly amusing to impede the house master," Seweryn said.

Doriel agreed with too much joviality in his voice. Alana didn't like to think about what had happened to them to make him hate Corwin so, but it was good to know.

In a manner childish for a young man so close to the end of his apprenticeship, Roark whispered to Seweryn, "You were right. He isn't jealous. At least not the way I thought." Her nephew turned away and vomited in a chamber pot. Spitting, he said, "It's much worse because there's no end to it."

*

PARALYZED BY SLEEP, ROARK FELT HIS SPIRIT leave his form and mingle with the memory of Corwin's hate. He felt lost within a dark cloud of the house master's rage and sorrow.

Light punctured his retinas. He feared he would vomit again. This time his corporal form would be left lying in a pool of his sick. He refused to allow the nausea to take him.

A long flat plain of salt stood before him. He took a step and broke through the thin crust spread across thick goopy liquid. Heat of an unseen sun beat upon him and evaporated the liquid forming a mist. Every step, he stumbled through the crust. Salt flew in the air.

Smoke and clanging metal swirled around him. Children screamed behind a wooden door. Oh no, not this day.

Flashing steel carved into the strong arm of his once lovely cousin, Saray. She parried, but a sword breaker caught her saber and snapped it in two. Another blade went through her chest. She drew her dagger and pierced the metal gauntlet that reached for the door. Then she spun and stabbed again. Her opponent fell.

She fell back on the door, then onto the ground. Blood flowed back to the Realm. Her bowels released and urine and feces spilled onto the ground. Her once blue eyes grew milky. Her flesh grew gray and rotted.

A male's scream echoed all around him. Roark turned as Corwin's hand reached through him and tried to hold Saray's spirit, but she left her rotting corpse. Now unfettered, she walked into the sun.

Saray had always known who sired her, but as Corwin never once visited her in the nursery, she never cared to know him. She was the Lady of the Keys of House Eyreid, Daughter of the Martlet Alana. She had fallen protecting the three youngest children of House Eyreid — one of which was Roark.

Saray's spirit stepped upon the Long Road. A path filled with dead things: millions of insects, hundreds of mice and squirrels, a few cats, dogs and a horse. All rotting flesh. Corwin tried to call for her, tried to reach for her, but she did not answer.

✳

ROARK OPENED HIS EYES. THOUGH SOAKED in sweat, his flesh was intact. *Saray walked with insects along the Long Road,* he thought with a shudder. He rolled over to see Eohan snoring on the bedroll beside his. Above them, in the sleeping chamber's only bed, Alana slept on her side, her sheathed sword beside her.

I didn't see the resurrection, only the Long Road! But his mind repeated: *Saray walked with insects.* As far as the Road was concerned, his cousin was the same as them. His mind spun. The priests claimed that if he lived by his vows, he would be resurrected as a noblewoman's son, but deep within his heart he knew that it was untrue. Eohan was a good man, a better man that Roark, and he was born a sausagemaker's son, then made a slave through no fault of his own. Kian was just a boy somewhere lost in the Realms.

We all are resurrected. It is chance, he thought. The Realms are too full of injustice for anything but random chaos to rule.

"Auntie," he whispered.

She opened her eyes. Out of habit, her fingers went to the hilt of her saber, but she did not unsheathe the sword.

"Do you believe the words of the priests?"

She shrugged. "The Realms are vast, and priests live cloistered lives, but it's good that we respect their wisdom. They know things we do not. We know things they do not."

"I think I've had a vision. I don't know if I saw the future, past, or present. I think the present. Or it started as the past, but became the present." Roark pressed his knuckles to his brow. His voice rose slightly. "How can I keep track of this madness?"

Beside him, Eohan mumbled in his sleep.

Alana touched his shoulder. "Do you need to speak of it, dearling?"

"I feel I better keep silent. I just need to know if I should take its wisdom over what the priests teach?"

"Well, I believe my foresight before the words of a priest." She tilted her head. "I may live to regret these words, but I learned to trust my foresight even before the words of my master."

Roark thanked her and laid back down, feeling Eohan's stability and warmth beside him. "It's good to be surrounded by friends. You were correct about that."

"Indeed," she whispered back.

※

Elizabeth Guizzetti

Chapter 13
Port Denwort in the Realm of Dynion

WHILE PORT DENWORT WAS A HUMAN city, peoples of all species moved about the market selling their wares. Guards wandered around in pairs, but they were lax in attitude and seemed uninterested in the petty crime around them. To the west was the slave block which was thankfully now empty. To divert Eohan's gaze, Alana asked, "What do you see, apprentice?"

"I've never seen such a population," Eohan said softly. "I almost don't know where to look."

"But you're hoping to see your brother running an errand."

"Yes, milady," Eohan said, slipping into his old habit of slurring common phrases into one word. On a different day, she would remind him, but today he needed a mother's gentleness, not a master's instruction.

The three Fairsinge rode slowly through the shop-lined streets. Above the shops were the homes of merchants. The wealthiest had multiple floors reaching to the sky. They turned down an eastbound street and stabled the horses and rented their lodging.

Alana felt easy as they waited for nightfall. They moved away from the square into a forest of stone houses and hedged gardens lining the streets on the hills until they came to a small, well-kept stone cottage with a clay shingled roof.

Alana touched Eohan's arm. "You and Roark must hold back."

"But milady…"

"Nyauail claims he is a shy one. We ought to listen," she said.

Eohan's hands trembled, and he chewed his bottom lip, but the boys hid in the shrubbery as instructed

She knocked on the cottage door. The small peep window opened and exposed a lich with a gruesome smile on his powdered white face and black charcoal around his piercing obsidian eyes.

"I seek Edar Candlewick," Alana said.

"For what?"

"I heard you have special remedies." She pulled at her collar and showed a hint of the weave.

The quiet was disturbed by grumbling and a creak of a lock being undone. The former human in scarlet robes sneered. He was easily three feet taller than her and wore a headdress which made him even taller. His breath smelled like death, and his chest did not rise and fall. Alana felt as awkward as a maid in a whorehouse under his gaze.

"Though you're rotting flesh, you seem healthy enough. What do you want? A potion to restore your faded beauty? Or a gift that stops aging all together?"

"Tempting, but no. I wondered about a boy in your house."

"I've no children." He tried to shut the door.

Alana grabbed his arm. "A slave?"

"I keep no servants at this time."

"You bought a ten-year-old Fairsinge boy named

Kian a few months ago."

"That whimpering creature was too weak for my needs. I discharged him within a week."

Keeping her voice soft, she asked, "Where is he?"

"I shouldn't know, now if you please..." Edar tried to push her out the door.

When she didn't move, he slapped her cheek. Though he struck her with an open hand, the blow felt like he was pounding her repeatedly with his fists. The air was filled with static. Alana knew if she lost consciousness, she was doomed.

She ran her fingers along her belt until she found a knife. Snatching it from its scabbard, she thrust her blade to the lich's neck. His menacing laughter choked, and he shoved her away.

"I want that name," she growled.

"For an old woman, your blood smells rich." He licked his lips.

"How much blood do you want for the name I want?"

"All of it."

"I have more knives."

He raised his hands. "A cup."

"Which cup?" Alana said.

He first touched a large crystal goblet.

"No."

Laughing, Edar plucked a small goblet from a cabinet filled with ceramics.

"You swear by your eternal life that in exchange for my blood you'll tell me who you sold the boy to."

"Yes." He set the cup on a table and gestured toward an upholstered bench. "Please sit. I rarely have guests."

"If you beat everyone when they enter, I see why."

"At my age, danger is everywhere." He pushed a bench to sit beside her. Perching on the chair, she sliced open the scar on her arm and leaned so the blood could fall into the cup.

"Is blood how you still walk?"

"Among other things." He licked his lips as blood dripped into the cup. "Would you like a demonstration of what the right blood can do?"

"Certainly."

She noticed movement outside the window and hoped the boys would not enter. This technology might be dangerous, but not so different than the blood magic that the Guild used in the binding.

The lich's silk shoes squeaked across the wood floor as he hurried into another room. His silks brushed across the floor. She remembered how loud Corwin was walking and wondered if he was trying to tell her something the younger Guild members wouldn't hear. But that was stupid, why would Corwin help her find a common boy? Unless he knew. Perhaps one of the birds told him.

Edar brought a beaker of blue powder and an empty pot. He plucked some herbs from his window garden. He added a bit of water and smashed the blue powder and herbs into a paste which he placed in the pot. "I keep two sets of cookware. That way my experiments are not tainted."

He hung the pot over the flame and watched the paste spark.

"And your slave boy?"

"Oh yes. Forgive me, my lady, I nearly forgot. I sold him to Master Grunkit."

"Grunkit?"

"The silk merchant who made this enchanting tunic and hat."

Keeping her voice light, she said, "His work is very fine."

The lich gently swirled the cup of blood and

drizzled it with his concoction, stirring it slowly. "We must be careful not to let it clot early." Edar drank, his carotid artery pulsed; his flesh grew flushed and pink.

She tried asking about his existence another way. "So the stories of the lich are true? The blood allows you to live?"

"I live without it, but blood allows me to enjoy the feeling of life." He took a step closer. "I would never have expected an aged woman such as yourself could make me young ... I'm willing to pay for more."

His long nails brushed against the wooden table as he reached for her.

She stood, putting the table between them. "And Kian's blood?"

"Too weak for my needs. He wept his strength away. But you..." Edar's pupils dilated as he stared at the wound on her arm. He sidestepped around the table and raised his empty right hand.

Before he could lunge, she slapped the cup out of his left hand. It tumbled to the ground. He howled in agony, knelt, and pressed his tongue along the grooves of the wooden floor, trying to get each drop.

Seeing his distraction, Alana escaped.

The boys waited for her outside. "Did you get all that?"

"Blood can make you live forever?" Roark asked, studying the front door of the lich's townhouse.

"Apparently, but I meant about Kian."

"He said there were potions to keep you young." Roark said, "You could live forever. You wouldn't have to worry anymore."

"It's nice you're thinking of me, but I'm not sure I'd want to live as that one does."

"It's odd he's so fearful when he can live forever," Roark said thoughtfully.

Worried her nephew seemed so taken by the lich,

Alana said, "Come. Let's rest and discover what we can about Master Grunkit."

＊

Chapter 14
Port Denwort in the Realm of Dynion

T HE NEXT MORNING, ALANA ARRIVED AT THE
Mayor's main gate in a blue linen gown the same
shade as her eyes, edged in black embroidery.
Following the human rules of etiquette, Alana allowed
the footman to take her hand and escort her inside.

The Mayor of Port Denwort, who was also the chief
spokesman of the Silk Merchants Guild, greeted her with
a small incline of his head. His brown, grandfatherly face
was surrounded by a cap of silver hair. His clean silks
and waxed mustache showed his concern of self. Though
as he crossed the small room to the upholstery, he used
a cane.

"You've a lovely home. Thank you for seeing me."

"Always delighted to see an elf-knight, especially
one who works for the Guild."

Alana sat on a plush, cushioned bench as the
footman poured goblets of sweet amber sherry. She
noticed a large tapestry of brown paths leading to a
central design of intertwined swirls of rich blue threads
surrounding black cherubim centered with an orb
within an orb within an orb. Below the circle patterns,

sparkling white and blue waterfall with figures hidden. If she moved her head, the figure disappeared, and a new figure appeared in a different place. A lich in Denwort and this tapestry wasn't an odd coincidence. She studied the mayor carefully, seeking signs of death. There were none.

In a weak, wheezy voice, the mayor said, "Ah, War Ender, I see my tapestry of The Water of Resurrection has caught your eye."

"Forgive me, sir, but you must take your medicine." The footman took a small blue bottle and poured a thick, blood-red liquid into the mayor's glass.

Alana smelled cobalt and herbs. The mayor's medicine was from the lich. Pointing at the tapestry, she said, "What a vibrant blue dye. The waterfall looks very realistic."

"It's one of a kind. The threads are said to come from the UnderRealm." The mayor winked.

Alana nodded. "You must have some brave merchants in this town to fib to the mayor."

He chuckled. "We do, we do."

She wanted to ask more about the tapestry but remained on topic. "I'm seeking Merchant Grunkit."

"Grunkit is a fine man." The mayor didn't stop talking, but beheld the nearest door and scratched at the coarse stubble on his throat. "He sells high only the best silks, and he always pays his dues on time. An honest man."

"I am certain he is." Alana ensured her voice remained calm and soft. She did not want the man to panic when he already showed stress responses.

"Why do you seek him?"

Alana decided truth was best. "Grunkit purchased a boy from Edar Candlewick. My apprentice, Eohan, is the boy's brother. We mean to buy him back. A life of a slave is no life for the brother of a Guild Apprentice."

The mayor scratched his neck again. "Is the Guild angry?"

"Not yet."

"Then, Grunkit routinely goes to the undertunnels of Si Na this time of year."

"And when will he return?"

"Maybe a fortnight, maybe a year."

"Do you know what route he took?"

"He headed north. He mentioned a few more stops in Dynion but didn't say where. He travels to the elf lands within six months for more silk. He's an honest merchant." As he spoke, his complexion grew brighter, and his wrinkles unfolded slightly.

"Do you know if he would travel to Daosith or Fairsinge territory?"

"I don't. I'm sorry, my dear, I don't mean to offend you, but outside of the occasional slave, I don't know the difference between the elfkin. All I know is you're a maiden knight of legend."

"It's been a long time since anyone called me a maiden." Alana laughed to show she was not offended.

The mayor drew in a great breath and laughed with her. The wheezing in his lungs disappeared.

"If he returns before I can find him, would you deliver a message to him?"

"Of course! I would be honored to be use of one of the great and mighty elf knight errants."

For a favor later, Alana read in his expression.

She stood and shook the mayor's hand. He stood without his cane. During the exchange, she stretched out her finger against his wrist to feel his fluttering pulse. He was alive. The blood potion could help one even who was not dead. *Interesting.*

✳

Trying to be faster than Alana's meeting, Roark raced to the lich's house. In witnessing the mayor's subtle transformation, he understood his vision of the Long Road. Panting, he pounded on the door until Edar Candlewick opened his little window.

"Second elf I've seen in as many days."

"I want a potion for my aunt ... I want her to live," Roark said, peering into the pale skin, still flushed.

"The elf lady with the wonderful blood?"

"Yes. We're related. If she has wonderful blood, then so do I."

"I don't sell my potions."

"You sell them to the mayor."

"I trade to be left alone."

Roark pressed his face closer to the door. "I'm unsure about the Guild's rule about allowing a lich to live. You play with dangerous technology."

The lich smiled, exposing yellowed teeth. "Yet, you want your aunt..."

"To be strong. To fight alongside me for many years yet. My mother is her sister. We have the same blood!"

The lich opened the door. He plucked a large clay goblet off his ceramics rack. "A portion for me, a potion for her."

Trying not to gag on his fear, Roark perched on the chair Alana sat upon earlier and rolled up his sleeve. The lich pressed a dirty nail into his smooth ivory skin until blood rose from his flesh.

*

ALANA SIGHED AS EOHAN JUMPED FROM HIS hiding place and ran to her. She would have to work on that with him.

"What did you find out, my lady?"

"Where's Roark?"

He stammered. "He saw something while we were watching ... and ...."

"Damn it. Come along." She sprinted back to the lich's home. If Edar Candlewick hurt her nephew, she would burn him out of existence. Eohan ran behind her, unable to keep up with her speed.

From down the street, she spotted Roark's auburn hair in front of the cottage, sitting on the stoop and staring at a blue glass bottle.

"Roark?"

"Auntie, I sold some blood." He tried to hand her a bottle, which sparkled in the bright sun, but it dropped to the ground.

"And that was foolish," she scolded. She collected the potion and set it in one of her small leather belt pouches. It was too expensive to waste.

"I want you to be strong."

"It's no gift if you weaken yourself." She turned to Eohan. "Help him. We need to eat."

"Eat?" Eohan echoed, his voice full of disappointment. "But what of Kian?"

"We need to eat to strengthen Roark. And yourself, unless you want to fall off your horse when you tire. We don't know Grunkit's exact route, and if we go the wrong way we're just putting more space between us. We ride within the hour."

"Yes, my lady," he sulked, but lifted the other apprentice.

Once they were at a table in the public-house, Alana tried to recreate the image in the tapestry, even though she knew charcoal in her old journal was a poor substitute for the threads so vibrant they sang.

"What's that?" Roark asked.

"A tapestry of The Water of Resurrections. Port Denwort has a surprising number of people trying to live forever."

"Live forever?" Roark repeated in a murmur, his voice showed he was still enchanted by that idea.

Alana cut off a chunk of her own beef and set in on his plate. "Eat, or you won't live to see tonight, young man, I'm still cross with you."

"You're the one who told me to believe in my foresight even before I heed the words of my master," Roark said.

"I knew I'd regret saying that," she replied.

✳

Chapter 15
Town of Havinberg
in the Realm of Dynion

THEY RODE HARD TO THE NORTH. DYNION was alive with noise from the wind rustling through the trees singing birds, calves and whelps frolicking. After dealing with two death-obsessed men and one apprentice who seemed too enchanted by the idea, Alana was glad to sense life. Yet, she was tempted by the potion in her saddlebag. The memory of the flush of life on the mayor's cheeks whispered for her to drink.

Roark was young and in good health. His blood loss did not seem to fatigue him. What kind of master would she be if she sacrificed her apprentice for herself?

The memory of the Edar's newly-found life in his dessicated body whispered for her to drink.

In deepening, blue twilight, they entered the next port town. Although a strong wind blew in from the south and made the water rocky, with the enclosed bay, Alana immediately recognized it as a safe harbor for large Interrealm ships.

Drumming her fingers on her legs, she said, "If Grunkit is leaving Dynion, this is where he might embark on an Expanse sailing ship. Or he might go further north?"

They rode to the past camped merchant wagons but did not see Grunkit Silks.

"Roark, find us a pasty shop." Alana tossed a coin his way. "Eohan, the horses."

The older boy drew water from the well, washed and watered the horses, taking the care to check for any saddle sores as he had been taught.

Alana approached the first merchant wagon where a family cooked supper on an enclosed stove. "Excuse me, I'm looking for a silk merchant named Grunkit?"

A man glanced up from slicing a loaf of coarse-grained bread and mouthed: Guild. His mouth hung open; his eyes wide.

Dishing out pottage, the woman said, "No one by that name here, but I've some silks fresh from Si Na."

"I seek the man," Alana replied.

"To..." the woman paused, looked back at her man with the bread, and ran her finger across her neck.

"Nothing like that. If you see him, let him know Lady Alana of the Guild seeks the boy, Kian, in his employment."

"The boy, Kian?" the man whispered. His complexion went ashen.

The woman ran his finger across her neck again.

"No." Gesturing towards Eohan, she said, "He is my apprentice's brother. We bring word of their mother."

"Oh," the merchant's voice sounded both relieved and disappointed.

"Tell him to go to the nearest Guild House with the boy. I'll be leaving a message in Dynion and Si Na."

"Yes, if I see him, I'll tell him."

Alana handed her a sovereign. "For your trouble."

Making her way back to the horses, Alana was glad to see Roark bought cheese and onion pies larger than her hand that looked more appetizing than the wet pottage and old bread the merchants ate.

✻

Elizabeth Guizzetti

Elizabeth Guizzetti

Chapter 16
In the Wilds of the Realm of Dynion

THE THREE FAIRSINGE RODE PASSED THE mud and reed huts of people so impoverished they couldn't live within village walls. They slowed as they crossed a wooden bridge, then turned east and followed a rough trail around the bridge abutment until the path dropped to the river's edge. The stench of poverty did not disappear as the party rode deeper into a lush, green forest filled with hanging moss and ferns.

The air grew colder. Eohan shivered. A growing stillness engulfed the forest. Without the birds and crickets' songs, the trees reached towards them menacingly. Or was Eohan imagining it?

He examined the entwined knots cascading down Alana's straight back rock with the horse underneath her. She glanced over her shoulder. Her blue eyes held a warning, her thin mouth set in a grimace. That wasn't what he wanted to see. She made a signal with her hands, though he didn't understand it, Roark did.

Roark pressed one word into his mind: Slavers. Eohan couldn't hold the tremble in his spine.

He rested his hand on the blade on his belt. In anticipation, his mind opened to the memory of his brother and mother being torn away from him. His mother had wailed his name. Her hand had gripped his arm so tightly when the slavers finally ripped them apart, bruises covered his wrist.

Alana and Roark were strong. They would fight. They would win.

*

ALANA SENSED THE HUMAN EYES IN THE forest and the unseen movement behind the trees. She sensed their clammy fear, sweat, dirt, and beer. Driven to unspeakable deeds to feed their children, these brigands were ravenous.

Twenty or so men slid down the clay hills.

Alana and Roark drew their sabers. Eohan pulled out his claymore.

Cloudy took a few steps back from the noise while Talia and Jaci moved forward. Afraid Eohan might falter in his first true fight, Alana rode in front, slashing her sword into the first man's neck and shoulder.

Screaming, he fell to the ground.

Three men grabbed Talia who reared in response.

A quarterstaff struck Alana's right shoulder with a crack. She shifted her sword to her left hand. With a strong swing, she disarmed the next man, then changed the direction of her stroke to the right and sliced another opponent across the face. He fell, shrieking.

Talia kicked, but somewhere more human hands appeared. Grasping at Talia's bridle and her waist, they pulled her off her horse. Paces away, she could see six or seven men on each of the boys. Eohan was pulled from his horse. She needed to reach him.

A man swung a quarterstaff towards Alana's brow,

she rolled away. The staff missed her and hit a tree. In his pause, Alana thrust her saber upwards into his stomach. A mortal wound although the man would not realize it until later. Alana fought on: parrying quarterstaffs and slashing her saber in the crowded space. She knew she could not keep her pace forever as her left arm tired.

Another human fell to the ground from her blade. And another. There was more than twenty. Where were they coming from? Women and older children joined the fray.

Alana spun, slicing her saber through the air. She felt the give of flesh and the crunch of bone, her saber stuck for a moment. Realizing she gave her opponent an opening, she let go of her sword and kicked the closest man in the groin. She backtracked and grabbed the sword once more. She slashed to the left as a man came at her. She misjudged his duck and clipped his forehead.

Blood stained the forest floor.

Out of the corner of her eye, she saw Roark pulled from his horse.

Alana rammed one of her assailants. Making some room, she parried away from a quarterstaff then sliced open another man's shoulder.

Eohan slashed his sword across a man's neck. Blood spilled down his chest. With an earsplitting battle cry, Eohan shoved him into Roark's blade, before attacking another man.

Roark was forced to backpedal as a blur of a man in chainmail thrust his longsword into the fray. Alana saw her apprentice's need and threw a knife into the man.

Eohan grabbed the next man's left shoulder and used his weight as a counterbalance to get out of the way while shoving him into a tree. He thrust his claymore through his opponent's mail. She needed to get to him before he made a mistake.

Hands aching, her swings were becoming erratic.

Every knuckle and joint ached.

A quarterstaff hit Alana's shoulder. Then the side of her head.

Blood dripping into her eyes, Alana could barely see her opponent, but she could smell the musty fragrance of someone who slept on dirt. Alana thrust her offhand dagger into his chest. As she extracted the dagger, it sang as it dragged against the chainmail. The last act of her opponent was his quarterstaff hitting her across the head, where she had been hit before. A ringing dull ache, she fell to the ground still holding her dagger. A second of blackness. An unending din.

Men's hands tugging on her purse, her belt, her weapons.

Her eyes fluttered open. She focused on the sparkling blue bottle in front of her. She kicked upward and connected with a man's groin. A man's grunt and the blue bottle fell on the ground. She grabbed it, popped it open and took a gulp, careful to cap it closed. She wouldn't waste Roark's precious gift.

Alana's esophagus was on fire. Heat moved outwards to her extremities. Heat became a hot coal searing her flesh as it localized on injuries. She screamed from the pain.

Still wobbly, her head aching, she shook the blackness out of her eyes and grabbed her sword off the ground. Youthful strength coursed through her veins. Feeling more alive than she had in years, Alana knifed the nearest man in his tendons. The man fell to the ground, screaming.

She jumped to her feet. She slammed her pommel into the top of the nearest man's head and crushed his skull inward.

She hadn't experienced such ease in sword work in nearly a decade. With every swing of her saber, she felt as if she were dancing in human blood. She made it to Roark.

Back to back, they thinned the battlefield until people struggled and tripped over each other to escape. Talia kicked the man who held Cloudy by the reins. Cloudy stepped on his leg, then bit the man who held Jaci's reins. The horses freed each other.

Five humans, four with quarterstaffs and one with a blade surrounded Eohan, whose claymore's sweeps were strong, but not connecting. Alana made several quick chest-level thrusts to either side, followed by a wide arc to disarm the closest opponent. On the return arc, she knocked another down.

She didn't want to stop. She wanted to kill them all. All on the battlefield and then all who let these people live in poverty. She sank her saber deep into a woman and enjoyed how the life drained away from her face. She imagined biting into her. She pushed the corpse to the ground. It was over.

Yet, her heart kept pounding with new found vigor, she wanted to chase each brigand down and observe the blood flow.

She forced her saber into its scabbard and watched the survivors run away. As they ought, the boys had already started to collect weaponry and coin from the bodies.

"My goddess, Aunt, that lump." Roark pulled out bandages.

Alana moved the bloodstained hair away from the raw flesh. "It's already closed. See to Eohan."

Roark scrubbed out Eohan's wound and stitched his side, but kept glancing at her.

"What is it?"

"Look in the mirror."

She opened her compact. The crease on her brow softened and the flush of her cheeks was the dew of youth. Scars faded. Even her hair seemed brighter auburn than before.

Roark's sacrifice made her a phoenix.

With my vast knowledge, if I was as strong as I was at thirty, I could finally change the Realms for the better. In her mind's eye, she saw herself slicing open her nephew's neck and drinking his remaining blood. Or maybe Eohan's. Her hand fluttered to her dagger.

Disconcerted, she shook every image of violence from her mind and put the potion deep in her saddlebag.

※

Chapter 17
In Uttalassus in the Realm of Si Na

Weeks became months in an unending nightmare of seeking one lost boy across several Realms. Alana refused to allow her apprentices to witness her depression, though after they went to sleep, she spent many nights lamenting her foresight.

Eohan grew despondent. He always behaved, but each night, he prayed until he wept, especially when they left Dynion, sought him in Daouail and then left that Realm and traveled to Si Na where they left their horses and went into the Uttalassus of Si Na, the home of the gnomes. In the relative safety of the Uttalassus, Eohan slowly learned to read and write. While his language skill in Telchinish was rudimentary, she saw improvement by instructing him to speak to innkeepers and merchants. Every night, Roark and Eohan sparred. Roark improved in his patience and kindness. The darkness of the Uttalassus sunk the travelers into despair as they sought Kian in village after village.

It took six months to find the wagon emblazoned with the words Grunkit Silks. Its lanterns burning thankfully bright.

Alana approached the party. "Master Grunkit, I need to speak with you!"

Though his man at arms was frowning, Master Grunkit spun around. His jovial ruddy face was set with a friendly smile, but his piercing blue eyes seemed to be seeking an angle. The woman beside him, likely his wife, was just as lovely, and her eyes seemed just as clever.

He inclined his head. Automatically the rest of the party followed suit. "An elf knight, what are you doing in the Uttalassus of Si Na?" His friendly bantering voice bore the thick accent of the Northern Dynion.

"I am Lady Alana Martlet of House Eyreid and a Guild War Ender. I seek an audience."

"Yes, of course! Come inside. Make a pot of tea, dearwife."

Unlike other merchants she had spoken to, he did not seem nervous to speak with a Guild War Ender. Alana remembered he had a lich for a client. The lich who had made her an antiaging potion out of her young nephew's blood. She ignored the wish to taste the potion again.

His clothes and those of his beautiful wife were of the finest silk damask and smelled of lemon and lavender. His wife set down a ceramic cup of tea for Alana first, then her husband and men, then served the boys.

"I'm sorry, but I sold that boy," Grunkit said.

Eohan stood, knocking the cup of tea to the floor.

"Eohan," Alana warned.

Her apprentice sheepishly asked for a rag to clean the mess. Mistress Grunkit brought him another cup and told him it was no trouble.

"Kian was a hard worker, but I found myself in arrears," Grunkit squeaked quickly, for the first time showing his nerves. "I had to do it or be enslaved myself! I had to protect my family. My employees."

"Who did you sell the boy to?"

"Lord Daeberos," the wife cried. "Please don't

hurt my husband! He was tricked into a game of chance."

"Lord Daeberos Royal Consort to Empress Ellryn of House Josael?"

"Yes. Daeberos might look like a kept man, but he is a shark."

Oh, sard. Alana thought. "Thank you, Master and Mistress Grunkit." She inclined her head and left. The boys followed.

Once outside of the lights from the wagon caravan, Eohan sunk to his knees. "We might as well give up."

Alana sat beside him and wrapped her arm around his shoulders. "No. While this is bad news, it is also good. Daeberos won't need to sell him for money, and probably can always use another house slave."

✳

ALANA RESTED DEEPER UPON HER PILLOW and opened her mind to the slave boy who worked in the kitchen. Pigeon-chested and lanky, one would not notice the family resemblance immediately, but it could be the right boy. She didn't want to go around killing Daosith nobility willy-nilly. It might accidentally start a war.

Seeking confirmation, she opened the boy's memories. She saw the slave ship. He stared towards the women's hold and listened to the screaming. "Leave my mama alone!" he cried until the overseer hit the bars with the whip.

On his pallet, the slave boy grumbled in his sleep.

She tried to go deeper, but those memories were lost in a fog. Ten years was too old to not remember his childhood.

"Mother," she whispered. An image of the boy's mother surfaced. A plump woman with strawberry blonde hair making sausages filled his mind. The image disappeared.

Black skeletons, demons covered in ash were surrounded by swirls of blue. This was the future, not the past. She was going the wrong way. Still, she could see the boy was intelligent as the man was in her vision. She looked at the brow shape and profile of his nose. Whether or not this Kian was truly Eohan's brother, this was the boy she would save.

"Soon a man arrives in bondage but is the way to freedom. When he arrives, find a weapon. Find a weapon," she whispered to the boy.

She opened her eyes. "Eohan, he was on your slave ship. His memories are too crowded with fear to read. I saw his mother making sausages. She had reddish blonde hair. Is that enough evidence?"

"Yes." The eagerness in Eohan's voice betrayed, he was too willing to believe his little brother was found.

"And if it is not your brother, you will pay anyway?" Alana asked.

"Pay?"

"The assassination fee," Alana said. "We must make sure this is on the up and up for Nyauail who brought us this information."

"Kill them?"

"Well, we don't want Kian to be a fugitive," Alana said.

"How will I get that type of money?"

"I'll ask my sister for a loan. We can set up a payment plan between us."

Roark put his hand out to help lift Eohan to his feet. "You'll like my mother and sister. They are innocent, never knowing what it was to take a life, yet both highly intelligent. They will help us."

✳

Chapter 18
Province of Eryedeir
in the Realm of Fairhdel

"Welcome to Eryedeir." Roark gestured towards the six-towered white castle pushed against the outcroppings to the sea below a small village surrounded by a stone wall, which looked as if it was carved out of the granite cliffs. Eagles soared on the funnels of wind. Above the birds, the sky sparkled from the three suns.

"Your mother's domain is beautiful," Eohan said, riding beside him.

"We like to make an entrance," Roark told him. They turned their horses into a small grove which led to a secluded beach.

Alana donned full court dress: the blue Martlet crested velvet justacorps worn to the knee, covering an equal length vest and matching breeches underneath. The coat was fitted throughout her chest, but the flared skirt, through the addition of gores and pleats, was loose enough to conceal weaponry. Two rows of pearl buttons and buttonholes lining the entire length coat, it remained unfastened. Even at home, a Martlet has her weapons.

Roark dressed in similar colors, though his court dress was simpler as proper for his age and rank. Still, his blue velvets were from a Great House. Eohan only wore the same Guild colors he had in Si Na, and they were wrinkled.

Alana pricked her finger with a needle and pressed the drop of blood on Roark's tongue. "My blood is yours, as long as I walk the halls of the Palace, no soul may harm you here."

"Will you tell them?"

"One set of bad news is enough for one day."

"Why would they harm Roark?" Eohan rubbed his hands over his tunic front.

"I didn't say they would, but we aren't bringing good news. Open your mouth." She pricked another finger and pressed it upon his tongue. "As long as I walk the halls of the Palace, no soul may harm you here either." She adjusted his tunic and straightened his collar. "In a few moons, we'll have to get you a new one. This won't fit much longer."

Jealous of his companion's physique, Roark regarded his own court dress. The daily rides and sparring trimmed Eohan's waistline, and each day Eohan gained weight in the shoulders and thighs. Roark hoped soon he too would gain muscle in all the right spots; right now, his body kept getting taller.

Alana never painted her face for court, and she didn't this day either, but she did take a sip of Roark's blood potion. He studied the actual transformation: her skin tightened around her jaw and eyes and the marks upon her hands disappeared.

"The potion is miraculous. I wish I obtained more."

Alana's eyes went dreamy, but then hardened in resolve. "I wouldn't take your blood, but we don't have any idea what to expect. My hope is it will be a joyous reunion, but we ask a sizable favor."

They mounted their horses and rode into town.

Merchants, smiths, and other trades stopped to bow as soon as they approached. Alana and her apprentices heard their names whispered and spread through the town. A few blocks from the square, builders constructed another block of two-story buildings.

"Good man, what is being built?" Alana asked one of the workers.

"Four new shops and homes above, Lady Alana. The Doyenne and Lady Ylynn's plan to help the refugees."

"Refugees?" Roark asked.

"Yes, the tale of your great deed proceeded you by many months, Master Roark."

A cry rang out over the square. "Lady Alana! Lady Alana is here!"

Three women raced towards them. Roark didn't recognize the common women, bowing in reverence and clasping his aunt's hands to their cheeks.

"I am glad to see you found safe shores," Alana said.

"Milady, every able adult ship did as you commanded," the wisewoman said. "We split to our respective Realms, but we each carried any weaker than us. Though a few went on, most of the Fairsinge traveled to Eryedeir, because, though we hear of the tales, we have never seen another Martlet. We petitioned the Doyenne. She and Lady Ylynn found us room in the garrison, gave us food." The women started weeping. "Now the Doyenne builds these homes, gives us loans to restart our shops. I opened an apothecary."

The women bowed again and tried to kiss their hands, their horses. More commoners surrounded them and did the same. Whispers of their arrival flew towards the castle. Finally, the three escaped up the limestone road, which spiraled over the curvature of the hillside until they came to three arching oak and iron gates. The sentries gave them wide smiles.

Inside the walls, the garden was ablaze with vivid red and yellow colored bracts. Stablekeepers, including a young girl, hurried to take the horses. Roark caught a glimpse of a scar on the girl's face before she knelt in the dirt and kissed Alana's boot.

"Child, rise. I am simply a Martlet, and I ride for the good of our people." Talia sidestepped so Alana could dismount without tripping over the girl.

The stablemaster hurried over, his face set in a frown, but before he arrived, Alana took the girl's hands and pulled her to her feet. The girl covered her scar with her hand.

"It gladdens my heart you are safe. Have you been well-cared for?"

"Yes, milady."

"And the Stablemaster, Stablemistress, and hands have been kind to you?"

"Yes, milady. Especially the Stablemistress."

"Good. I won't keep you from your duties any longer, dear one." She handed Talia's reins to the girl, who clicked her tongue and led the horse into the barn.

"Forgive Adana's impetuousness." The stablemaster's eyes darted from side to side, trying to decide who to look at. He eventually decided on the ground. "I will chastise her for disturbing you if you wish it."

"I assume Idana does not stop every person of my House."

"No, milady."

"And she's a devoted hand?"

"Yes, milady."

"Then there is no reason to chastise her. I am gladdened the poor soul found a place. She is younger than I realized." She pointed at his chest. "Your heart would've broken if you had seen how I found her. I slaughtered him gladly."

"I would've liked to squeeze his neck if I could, milady, as would my good wife," The Stablemaster said. "My wife even forbade the hands to make the girl the butt of their jests as is often the case with green apprentices."

"Bring your wife to me."

The Stablemaster bowed, turned almost stumbling over his feet, and ran inside the carriage house. Seconds later, the Stablemistress approached with husband and bowed deeply, wiping her hands upon her heavy woolen breeches. "Lady Alana, Master Roark. Master of the Guild," she said in turn to each of them.

Roark couldn't believe the commoners thought Eohan part of the gentry — though he supposed he might earn the title of War Ender.

"Do you care for Idana?" Alana asked the stablemistress.

"Yes." The woman paused and, as if she made out the reason for the questions, said, "Fear not, though Idana's green, she's devoted to the horses and hunting dogs."

"Good. But I ask you one thing more."

"Which is?"

"As she has no mother to speak for her when she is ready – and I realize it might be a few years yet – speak for her if she chooses to be married? You will ensure a good match?"

The stablemistress's eyes lit up in understanding. "Of course, we wouldn't let one of our hands be taken in by some smooth lordling or ladyling that comes to visit House Eyreid. No disrespect to you or your friend, Master Roark."

"None taken," Roark replied.

"We know you're true gentlemen to save the girl and all the others as you did. She told us the story many times. How a dark-haired slave boy — I don't think she knew you were a Guild Master, milord — rowed the ship even though waves tossed it to and fro. She never knew what happened to you, only you disappeared with Lady Alana, and another young man whom we knew by her description was Master Roark.

"But we know the type you're worried about, Lady Alana, and we'll be keeping an eye upon any suitors that come this way. It is kind of you to ask after the girl."

Alana handed the stablemistress three gold sovereigns. "Take this for the child. You may not think you need it, but my apprentices are both growing out of their boots."

As they walked away, Roark saw Idana peek out of the stable after them. He wondered why his aunt hadn't chosen the girl to be his friend since she seemed to be so taken by her now.

Keeping her voice low, Alana replied, "Because, dearling, I didn't know if she would survive. She was so ill-used and malnourished ... I wasn't even sure of her age. If you would like an additional companion, assuredly she would make a fine groom, but I shudder to think of that sweet child in battle."

The carved wooden doors of the inner keep opened into the Great hall Beside him, Eohan gasped.

The entire room danced in light from the stained-glass windows. Fireplaces were set every ten paces or so, and between the fireplaces were groups of portraits hung by generation. Some faded and restored many times, the previous few generations brighter.

In Roark's generation, only three portraits hung upon the wall. His elder siblings and his cousin, Saray, looked down upon them. Their youthful, fresh faces each painted upon the earning of their title. *How many more years until I join them?*

At the head of the hall sat his mother upon her throne and his family surrounded her. Roark wanted to remember her face or feel love for her, but his heart felt achingly empty as she looked upon him with piercing blue eyes that matched his own. She was older than Alana by a decade, but since she rarely saw the sun, her skin was only marred by crow's feet. Her long, silver curls spilled down her back. She stood tall in her perfect white velvet gown which opened under her full bust and exposed layers of satin and scalloped, sparkling lace. "So my sister and son have returned?"

Alana, Eohan, and Roark bowed.

Laraena opened her arms. "My son."

He crossed the steps into his mother's outstretched arms, though he didn't know if she truly wanted to embrace him or was doing it for the approval–or disapproval — of the court. There was always something. *Lowest Realm, she might have a dagger to stick in his back.* Happily, Roark discovered she didn't. Laraena looked upon Alana but slipped a note into Roark's pocket. He smiled. It would have been worth being stuck to feel his mother's embrace.

"I return your own blood and seek your counsel in a matter of great importance, Doyenne."

"What is this matter?"

"As the other refugees were, this boy, Eohan son of Aedell, was taken from Fairhdel shores and found enslaved in a distant land. I made him my apprentice. Now we seek his lost brother."

"That seems like an insignificant errand for a Martlet," Roark's father said. As was expected, Roark's father wore house colors in his velvet coat and a taciturn smile. Roark's eldest sister, Ylynn sat at their father's side and was not smiling at all, and nor was her husband. Roark's brother stood on the right at the house priests section. Roark's heart grew colder; his mother might embrace him, but they would not.

"What is Roark's involvement in this?" Laraena asked.

"Eohan is my friend, my Lady Mother." Roark realized the truth of his words. Other than Alana, Roark never trusted anyone, but he trusted Eohan to stand beside him.

"But he is a commoner?"

"Yes. It is my honor to serve our people as Martlets have done before me," Roark said, his voice growing in passion as he spoke. "All our people. The Martlets have served only the nobility for far too long, and our people are poorer for it. We allow slave ships to ravage our shores and find sanctuary in our cities."

Laraena stepped away from Roark and studied him carefully. "You are quite improved, my son."

"Aunt Alana sensed his importance — his future importance to me and this House," Roark said.

"How so?"

"She had a vision."

Laraena turned back to Alana "I suppose you don't want to spoil the surprise for the young men."

"No."

"Then walk with me. Ylynn come along. Roark, introduce your friend to your father and brother and cousins."

Saddened to see his mother leave, Roark itched to see the note in his pocket. He waited. He was good at waiting. He introduced his friend to his relatives as he was bid.

※

AS THEY ENTERED THE CENTER CHAMBER, Alana detected the sharp odor of vinegar and noted the plastered walls and painted floorboards were freshly cleaned. Alana opened the panel in the servant's corridor. Empty. Ylynn closed the thick oak door and lit three candles and set them on the table. The candlelight created strange shadows, just as the fire in her vision. She thought of the little girl that shared her name.

Laraena sat down beside her harp and began to play loud enough that no one could hear their words, soft enough for conversation. "What do you need, Alana?" she asked.

"Money to kill Kian's masters. We want to put out a contract on them. Keep it legal."

"You believe this boy and his brother are that important?"

"Eohan's destiny is to be a War Ender. Eohan and Kian will be the protectors of one of your granddaughters."

"One of my daughters?" Ylynn asked.

"I can't be sure. The girl looked very much like Roark."

"Roark's inclinations remain unchanged?" Laraena asked.

"Yes."

"How will Roark sire a child, much less a child with a maternal line of substance?" Ylynn asked. "If he sires a child, will she be in line for Doyenne?"

Alana sighed. Doyennes and Doyennes-in-training often thought the world revolved in court. "Your daughter is perfectly safe, Lady Ylynn. All I saw was Roark scolding a frightened child. Eohan rocked her to sleep. I couldn't hold the vision, but the child is on the road at a tender age. She must be the next generation's Martlet."

"Why does she wander so young?"

"The child has noticeable foresight." Alana gestured to her own brow. "Due to our training, your son's gift is no longer latent. Ahh, perhaps that explains it."

"How so," Laraena asked.

"Perhaps you and Ylynn allow Roark to sire a

child in the Martlet line to ensure the gift does not fade in House Eyreid."

Laraena ran her fingers one at a time up the harp strings.

"Funding you might endanger our House. Eryedeir has remained in peace for two centuries, we do not want a war with the Daosith," she said.

"Rulers often have more than one enemy, as you well know," Alana said. "Eohan will pay for assassination, and if we fail, it is he who will shoulder the blame. I ask for funds to save this boy, so Eohan doesn't run off half-cocked. And this child of our house has a devoted protector."

"Does my son fall early?"

"No," Alana hoped this might wait, but the subject had arisen. Now was the time to tell it. "Roark will fall aside in his training. He will be an assassin or worse try to wander without steady employment from the Guild. He does not have the temperament to end wars. I have foreseen it. I ensure others will catch him and the child."

Laraena rubbed her hands together. "I grant you this, but I will ask more of you, Sister. Once you save Kian, I will fund an expedition to save the other children. Find word of deaths or buy the children and bring them to these shores. My new citizens miss them."

"Happily."

✳

ONCE AWAY FROM THE HOUSE AND ON THE road, Roark slipped the note from his pocket.

Son,
Our holdings are richer for your defiance. The refugees

tell a wild story that gets greater with every telling, but I fear for you both if this story leaves our borders. My heart overflows with pride at your accomplishments.

            - Mother

✳

Elizabeth Guizzetti

Chapter 19
Guild House of Olentir
in the Realm of Fairhdel

"WHAT IS THIS?" CORWIN SCREECHED, his spittle landing upon Alana's cheeks.

She had known the House Master would take news of the job badly. She planned for it; she left her apprentices in a private chamber and faced him alone. He might try to hurt them to hurt her.

"Lord Daeberos? Are you insane?" His fists landed on his counting table.

She wanted to rail against the injustice of the Realms, against slavery of their people. However, the morality of slavery was an old argument between them. She wouldn't reach Corwin by those words.

"What could you possibly hope to gain by doing this?"

"Nothing, but it's within the law for Eohan to legally pay for a contract and request I plan the job as a training exercise for my apprentices."

Alana's words were caught in her throat by Corwin's hands squeezing tightly.

Bringing her left arm up, she tried to knock his

hand away. With more power than his wizened body should hold, he backed her into the stone wall behind her.

"I should have you crucified." His hot breath reverberated through her ear. "Tell me why that boy is so important to you ... for any reason at all. Our years together ... our child's death. It doesn't matter as long as you tell me before I mercifully strangle you and hide your body within the catacombs. You're an old War Ender, no one will look too hard."

Alana had instructed her apprentices to ride if she didn't return to them within an hour. She wished for the blood potion, but it wasn't with her. It remained deep in her saddlebag.

He squeezed his fingertips harder but left room on her throat so she could speak.

Unwilling to show her fear, Alana sighed. "Corwin, I have never touched one of my apprentices in that manner, nor will I. You know this."

"Then why is that hedgeborn boy important to you?"

"I saw him in a vision," Alana said.

Corwin let go of her neck but held her fast against the wall. "Of?"

Choosing her words carefully, she said, "A child who bears my name will be gifted with foresight. I only know if Roark stands alone that night, his circle of protection will collapse. Something would have broken through. In my vision, Eohan listened to her, though she was quite small and frightened."

"Why?"

"He is a War Ender. Just like you were once; he listens to all sides."

Corwin was not yet convinced.

"The next Alana of House Eyreid will be the War Ender we hoped so many others would be."

"The type of War Ender I want, or you want?"

"Unknown."

She expected anger; she was surprised by his sadness. "Why couldn't you see such things about our Saray?" he asked.

"I didn't choose our child's fate," Alana whispered. "You want the Guild to be respectable again, to have stories and sagas told and retold. This girl is your chance."

He released her. "If you would have told me before, I'd have saved you the coin. The empress's granddaughter has been nipping at the throne for years. Too late now to trick her into hiring the Guild."

"If you'd stop threatening me and my apprentices like a jealous fiend, we might enjoy each other's confidence once more."

Corwin didn't answer her; he only chuckled as he turned away. But before his withered form disappeared through the walls of darkness, the chuckle fractured into a sob.

His sadness tugged at her heart, but she was too old for regrets.

Thirty-seven years ago, Corwin happily placed Saray in House Eyreid with his name and nothing else as was proper. Their daughter had died in battle. She presumably had since resurrected. Nothing could bring her back no matter how much each of them wanted it to be different.

*

Elizabeth Guizzetti

Chapter 20
The Great House of Josael
in the Realm of Daouail

KIAN IGNORED THE STENCH OF BLOOD OVER lingering floral perfumes as he carried the tray of wine for the Empress and Royal Consort into the Great Hall. Each time, he smelled blood his mind revolted to a different time. A time that didn't matter. All that mattered was he didn't spill the wine.

Comfortable in the court's opulent surrounding, the Empress and Royal Consort listened to the twittering gossip of the courtiers. The clinking of glasses. The crackling of the fire. The fluttering of ringed hands and swish of layered silks. It was always the same. Most importantly, the nobles would ignore Boy as long as their wine glasses were kept filled.

A new Fairsinge slave was chained in the corner. At first glance, this new slave looked like his lost brother. His massive body, unlined brow, and black hair were covered in sweat and dirt. His laced back was dark from the sun. He was probably used to traverse the Expanse or perhaps he was used for the arena. His tri-pointed ears folded flat against the side of his head, but his eyes were not broken. He thought again of the brother he once had. The old woman from his dreams whispered, "Find a weapon."

Kian shook the memory from his head. *The old woman didn't matter. Nothing mattered.*

The nobles' youngest grandsons threw pieces of bread at the new slave and dared each other to touch his raw back. They laughed as the slave shoved the food in his face before the bored guard yanked on his collar.

Kian thought of his lost brother once more. *No. No. No.*

Kian refilled the wine glasses — emptying the carafe. He slid down the lime-plastered hallway through the wooden archway that led to the kitchen. Unbalanced by the blistering memory of his family, but careful not to be caught, he drained the dregs into his throat hoping to forget.

He tried to hold on to his brother as the slavers ripped them apart. Eohan had been thrown into the cell bound for the arena. The slavers threw him into a hold with other children. Women were in the cell across from him and chained to bunks. He often heard the women screaming as the sailors visited them.

He needed to escape. The old woman from his dreams whispered again, louder this time, "Find a weapon."

Kian prepared another tray. Steel glimmered at the bottom of a washbasin. Without thinking, he grabbed a knife. Heart pounding, he slid it into his waistband, hoping Cook had not noticed.

Once in the servants' corridor, fearing the knife might loosen and slide down his pant leg, he ripped the cuff of his pant and tied the blade to his thigh. He glanced over his shoulder; no one was there. He took a sip of wine, this time not just the dregs.

Lowering the cup, he thought he saw a shadow in

the corner creeping up the servant's corridor, but when he looked again it was gone. Kian made his way back to the Hall and waited at his station until the Empress and the Royal Consort took to their bed.

Cook did not see the missing knife before he retired. Finally, the castle was quiet as the servants and slaves finished their chores. He retired to his mat on the floor.

He listened as shadows of slaves lay upon their mats. A few engaged in sexual congress. Thankfully tonight, no one approached him. He waited until snoring surrounded him. He held his breath as he sat. His heart pounding, he crept out of the kitchen and down the hall, careful his footfalls did not make a sound.

In the dim, empty great room, the stench of his blood and sweat rose into his nostrils as he approached the brute.

"I'm a slave like you," he whispered quickly in Daosith. The man stared at him in reply. Something about this man's hazel eyes which enveloped Kian with a sense of familiarity.

"I can't escape on my own, but together we could. I'll get you out of the castle if you get me through the Expanse."

The brute nodded. "I am called Eohan."

"I-I'm just called Boy, but Kian's my name, and Eohan was once my brother's name," Kian said in Daosith.

Eohan said something in their mother tongue that Kian didn't understand, then gestured at the lock.

"Yes." Kian bobbed his head, though he wasn't sure that he could do it. Using the knife, he fiddled with the lock. He had never picked a lock before. The inner workings wouldn't move. Tears sprang to his eyes.

"Calm yourself," Eohan said in their mother tongue. His voice was rich and tender. The voice of his elder brother resonated in his mind, but Kian pushed the thought away. To be reunited with his brother was a fanciful dream. The Realms were cruel. He wanted a drink.

The knife jumped from the lock and slid across Eohan's skin. Blood rose from the wound.

Kian pinched his eyes shut, expecting a blow.

"Stay calm. Keep working on it. I'll keep watch. Feel the tumblers. That's good. You have plenty of time."

"No. We only have a little bit of time before Cook wakes. You don't know ... you don't know..."

"Remain calm." Serenity echoed in Eohan's deep voice.

Kian wiped his face on the tail of his dirty shirt. Fearing a guard passing by, or that a slave might awaken, he glanced over his shoulder. No one was there. Besides Eohan's soft voice, the only sound was the clock that ticked loudly and sounded on the half hour. Sweat poured down his back. Every moment, he was sure someone would wake in the servants' corridor and notice his pallet was empty. They would come looking for him. They would find him with Eohan. If he was lucky, they would only beat him.

"You're doing fine," Eohan said. "Feel the tumblers. This lock's a simple thing."

With Eohan's guidance, Kian felt a click. It snapped open. Tears of joy streamed down his cheeks. Eohan removed the metal cuffs and stood without making a sound as he set the chains to the ground.

Kian might have thought that was odd if the sight in front of him didn't terrify him. Unchained, the man towered over Kian. This Eohan could not be his brother. His brother had been big and strong, but he had been a boy. This man was huge.

"Let's go," Eohan said rubbing the cut on his wrist.

Kian hurriedly led Eohan back to the kitchen.

He put his finger to his lips and pointed towards Cook sleeping on a pallet in his alcove.

Eohan nodded.

Glancing behind him, Kian opened the wooden panel in the wall. He crawled into the grease-lined garbage chute. Nearly overwhelmed by the smell of rotting food, bile rose in his throat. He tried holding his breath. He glanced back. Eohan pulled himself along, filling the entire chute.

Kian got a whiff of fresher air as he popped his head out. The world was painted in the dim blue of night. No one noticed they were missing yet.

He grasped on the rocks above the chute and tried to maneuver his legs below him. He tried to slowly lower himself to shorten the drop to the rock below.

Eohan grabbed his wrist and pulled his hands away from the stone.

Panic rose in Kian's throat, but Eohan only lowered him further.

"Ready?" Eohan whispered and let him go. The red stone stung the soles of his feet. He bounced around to get the sting out. Eohan lowered himself and dropped beside him.

"This way." The boy showed Eohan a path around the Daosith village. From this distance, the palace that had been his home was beautiful. Its spiraling towers appeared to sprout straight out of the reddish-brown stone cliff and arcing domes spread out like flower petals unfurling towards the moon. "I won't miss it," he whispered, but his heart wondered if that were true. He had been sold so many times.

Kian hurried up the hill to the river. He didn't know if he should laugh or cry, but his thighs burned with each step and mud oozed between his toes. He didn't dare stop.

The big man's face was set in a frown, but he

walked without complaint. They climbed the second hill. Kian's lungs felt as if they might burst, but Eohan breathed regularly.

"Let's wash this dreck off," Eohan said.

"What if they come?" Kian asked. "We sometimes come here to fish."

"The sun hasn't risen yet, and we won't stay long."

Kian was careful to stay out of arm's reach of the big man. However, Eohan only jumped into the water with a slight yelp. Shivering, he wiped away the grease as best as he could and plunged his dark hair in and out with a few wild grunts. Muttering about the cold, he pulled off his ragged pants and beat them against a rock.

Kian did the same. Now naked, Kian pushed down his feelings of shame. He didn't want the man to judge him still a boy. Or see his scars from the lash. Or know how other slaves touched him in the darkness. He wanted this Eohan to be his lost brother, but he feared his brother's shame of him. It was better if this Eohan wasn't his brother.

The man didn't so much as glance at him. If anything, he was still annoyed by the icy water. He gingerly pulled on his ragged pants.

"We should drink." Eohan cupped his hands and drank his fill.

Kian did the same.

He led the way up the next hill. Then the next. They followed the river for miles until it opened into a deep clear pool. "Let's rest here," Eohan said and pushed leaves into a pile next to a stone which he reclined upon.

"Is it true Fairhdel has three suns?"

"Have you been a slave so long?"

"I don't remember my home. I think I do, but then I don't. My memories scald me."

"Fairhdel has three suns," Eohan said with a deep sadness in his voice and picked at a callus on his hand.

✻

ROARK SILENTLY ASCENDED THE RED STONE wall to a shuttered window. He climbed into the marks' room, slipped behind the thick curtain, and waited for the Empress and Royal Consort to retire for the evening.

This would be an interesting experience. A noble assassination. *What a job for an apprentice!*

Still, watching the lad creep over to Eohan, "save" him and escape the castle opened an old wound. His siblings wouldn't have saved him from slavery and paid to have the old master's killed. Nor would he for them. Of course, it had never come up.

Finally, the marks entered the chamber. Roark wondered why such wasted creatures hung on to life. Watching the elderly couple undress, he observed their sluggish movements, shaking hands, and their sagging, sunken skin. He could not let that happen to him. He did not want to ever grow old. He didn't want Alana to grow old either.

Soon the couple's snores became quite regular.

With a gloved hand, Roark silently extracted a dead frog. He split open its skin and cut out its liver. He put the rest of the frog back in his pouch. Roark sliced the liver in two. He timed when they opened their mouths naturally and slid the liver onto the tongues of his victims.

The Empress sat up in terror, but could not shout for help as her throat closed around her words. Her struggle awoke her consort. He screamed and tried to pound her on the back. He began choking. It was over quickly.

Roark checked for a pulse from the artery in their necks. Both were still. He studied their dead eyes and checked their throats for traces of poison. As it should, it completely dissolved.

Roark strangled the Empress purposely to cause bruises. He broke the bottle over her head. He quickly grabbed a few valuables and ripped the curtains. Then he broke the window shutters and threw the Consort's body to the landing below. The new "brute" was supposed to take the blame.

Roark hurried down the steps to ensure Kian wasn't still fiddling with the lock. Seeing the brothers had escaped the castle, he climbed out a window and down the castle walls on the river side. Careful to stay out of sight of the village, he silently jogged to the rendezvous.

*

EOHAN WISHED ALANA AND ROARK WOULD hurry. Kian was damaged. Perhaps beyond repair. It had only been a year, but Kian did not remember him or his former home. He seemed so small and thin. Too thin. *Perhaps it was best if he never knew they were brothers.* The thought left a lump in Eohan's throat.

He wiped leaves and dirt off as well as he could, then headed down to the river where Kian tied his knife to a stick and stabbed at the water. Hemmed in by boulders, the riverside rendezvous location felt safe enough. *Where was Alana?*

Kian backed away from Eohan. "I didn't catch anything yet," he admitted with his hands up.

"We had a deal. You get us out of the castle, I'll get us out of this land."

"What will happen then?"

"What do you mean?"

"Where will you take us?"

Eohan smiled sadly. "I guess you can come to the

Guild with me."

"The Guild?"

"A place where you can work."

"You'll sell me?" Kian's voice sounded hollow. Dead.

"The Guild does not accept slaves, but you can apprentice there," Eohan said. "Or perhaps I can take you to a village."

A whistle interrupted him.

"It's about time," Eohan snapped.

Roark entered the grove. "Welcome to our party, Young Master Kian."

He rummaged through his bag for an unguent, bandages, and an oily suspension.

"You would call me by my name?" Kian asked.

"And I shall call you the brother of my friend."

Roark dabbed the unguent over the re-opened wounds on Eohan's back and the cut on his wrist that Kian accidentally gave him. He uncapped the bottle with his teeth and knocked back the suspension to dull the pain.

Still not looking at Eohan, Roark handed him first a linen undertunic and then black wool.

"Allow me to reintroduce you to Eohan, son of Aedell, the sausagemaker, and Cadfael smith in the village of Aberfoel, now a Guild Apprentice training to be a War Ender. We've searched Realm after Realm for you." Roark bowed to Kian. "I'm Roark, Martlet-in-training of House Eyreid, Son of Doyenne Laraena and Lord Aldan, Younger brother to the Great Lady Ylynn. Guild Apprentice training to be the Assassin of the Realms."

How could Roark say all that in one breath? Eohan thought. He did not like the way Roark's eyes were focused on his little brother.

"I dreamt of a lady. She told me you were coming. Is that Doyenne Laraena?"

"No, my aunt, Lady Alana, the greatest of all Martlets."

"So noble Fairsinge really wander around saving people?"

"We are real." Alana approached, followed by the horses. "The job was completed cleanly. You both did well."

"Job?" Kian asked.

"He hired me to kill the Empress for the distress she caused you," Roark said.

"She didn't cause me distress; she ignored me."

"Never the less, she and the Royal Consort are dead," Alana said.

Kian flinched at the words "Royal Consort." Eohan wanted to embrace his brother, but Roark patted his shoulder.

"She died without pain, but I poisoned him and threw him out the window."

"Good. I hated him. He was a ... bad ... man."

"I'm sorry I didn't tell you immediately, but..." Eohan was too overwhelmed by emotion to speak. This wasn't how he expected his brother to react. The coldness behind his eyes was not like him. He used to smile and sing.

"It was indispensable to ensure you weren't broken," Alana said, "I inserted a subliminal message into your dreams. If you hadn't wanted to escape — if you succumbed to slavery — you wouldn't have been brave enough to steal the knife and free Eohan."

"What would have happened to Eohan if I hadn't come?" Kian asked.

"I would've picked the lock, and left you to your fate," Roark said.

"So this is fated?"

"I don't know if anything is fated, but we are creatures of habit, and we do what we do. I set something in motion when I rescued Eohan — and as his future is now bound up with Roark's — we needed to rescue you, too. You cannot return to the castle." Alana said. "Will you come to the Guild or should we find you an apprenticeship in a village somewhere?"

"I don't know. I would be free?" Kian asked.

"As free as any of us," Roark said. "We vow to serve, and that vow is sacrosanct, but we are paid well."

Kian smiled at the nobleman's words. His hazel eyes became full of resolve.

"Then the Guild is where I want to go," he said.

Eohan's heart plunged into the pit of his stomach. Alana had warned him that his little brother might be different boy than the one he knew. She had been right. The Kian who laughed easily, smiled and sang was gone.

✳

Chapter 21
A cottage in a wood,
somewhere in the Realm of Daouail

COVERED IN SWEAT AND HEART RACING, Kian paced the sleeping loft. Fresh rushes were spread on the oak floor muffling the sound of his feet. The linen-covered bed was fit for a noble son of a noble lady, not a house slave. He dare not lay in it beside his brother. Roark and Lady Alana were below near the hearth.

Outside the window, large clouds moved across the dark sky. Kian couldn't see the double moons. His pacing became faster. He scratched his chest.

Alana seemed kind enough. She had given him an extra bowl of pottage and half her cake at dinner. Kian suspected she studied him, read his mind. *What if she told Eohan? Eohan would be ashamed of me. Hate me.*

The need for wine overwhelmed him.

Alana provided him with fresh clothing, but his hands slick with sweat, he didn't dare touch them. He couldn't get the smell of garbage off his body. That's what he was: garbage.

He climbed down the ladder. He passed the

hammock where Roark slept. The bed was empty. Where was Alana? Maybe she went to the pot or to check on the horses. He slid his feet across the floor to remain unheard.

He went to the cupboard in the back of the cottage and looked through their supplies: jars of vinegared fruit, a round of cheese, dried sausage.

Behind him, Alana cleared her throat. "You won't drink wine, mead, whiskey or beer for now. Our well is clear, and the water is fresh."

He jumped. "I didn't see you there."

She appeared much smaller without her layers of armor. Weaker. Her face bore wrinkles on her brow and crows-feet around her eyes; her bare arms were covered in scars. "Don't bother lying to a mind reader, scroggling. To protect your soul, you allowed darkness to descend over it. If you do not waste your brother's sacrifice, I see great things in you. Water or milk. Nothing else." The old witch turned around, her faded braid swinging behind her. "Come."

The need for drink pounded in his head. "Lady Alana, I'm sick."

"That's why I brought you to this safe house." Alana put her arm around him. He pulled away, but she held him. "You feel the call of wine, but you must fight it. You are young, but there will be more sweats. Perhaps vomiting. Insomnia. Paranoia. The Guild has been quite aware of this phenomenon for some time, but if you come to them in a weakened state, your reputation might be harmed."

"What do I do?"

"I'll tell you a story if you like …"

She set Kian on her bed. He cringed away, but all she did was lay a wet cloth upon his brow. "I won't ever harm you, child. I'm sorry you were hurt by people of loose morals and depravity."

Not wanting to see the pity in her eyes, Kian turned his head away. "What will Eohan say when he knows?"

"He does know." Her voice surrounded his mind.

"Everything?"

"Most things. He was there when I dictated my vision of you."

Kian stared at the ceiling, unblinking. "I once was the son of a sausagemaker, then I was a slave that no one wanted. Now I stand on the edge of chasm ... Gods I want a drink!" he shouted and kicked at her. "I need one! Just one!"

Alana stopped him by the strength of one finger on his sternum. Unable to sit up, Kian spit, but only accomplished getting spittle on his chin.

"I can offer you a life in the Guild, or you can choose an apprenticeship with a butcher, but I won't let you drink tonight or tomorrow or the day after."

Kian stared at the two young men who approached. Kian wanted to bite Roark's neck and let those blue eyes fade to a milky white. He wanted to stab his brother for leaving him to his fate. And he wanted to murder the old witch.

He kicked upwards. "Eohan, help me!"

His so-called brother pressed Kian's thrashing legs into the mattress. "We can't let you drink wine tonight."

"You're hurting me," Kian cried out.

In response, Eohan loosened his grip. Kian saw his weakness and pressed upwards. Kian tried to bite into his brother's arm; Eohan slapped him away.

Though it hadn't even stung, Kian laughed hysterically. "You aren't my brother! My brother would never hit me."

"I'm sorry. I didn't mean to." Eohan's dark eyes flitted away. He almost let go again. This time Kian would bite him.

"Roark, help Eohan," Alana ordered.
"I'll kill you, witch!"

*

WITH THE OLDER BOYS HOLDING KIAN, Alana dug into her saddlebag. She found the half-drank blood potion, now thick and clotted. She shook the bottle until the liquid moved and uncorked it. The smell of blood tempted her senses. She suddenly didn't want to waste it on a common boy, it was hers. Her own nephew had sacrificed himself for it.

Eohan grunted and Roark swore under his breath.

She glanced over at the three boys. She had to help Kian. Fear and self-hatred had grown into weeping lesions of poison dripping into Kian's soul. Malnutrition and wine stunted his height. Alana wasn't sure how to help him, but minimally he needed sleep.

Hoping the potion would take away his pain, she pressed the bottle of Roark's blood to the boy's lips. She didn't know if it was the taste or the pressure from the bottle, but Kian accepted it willingly. He drank deeply until only drips coating the glass remained.

"I don't know if this will last long enough to get him through the call of wine, but perhaps it will curb the worst of the cravings," she said.

Though she tried to keep her voice calm, Alana heart sank. She wasted her nephew's precious blood on a common boy. Her soul ached for the loss until the boy screamed and grabbed his head. He rolled on his side and curled up tightly, gasping for breath. Alana feared she poisoned him.

Suddenly, Kian straightened. The circles under the boy's eyes faded. The sheen of sweat melted away. He stopped trembling. Alana put a wet cloth onto his chewed lips which were already showing signs of self-healing.

Eohan quickly set a blanket on his brother than ran a rope across Kian's torso and tied it to the oak bed frame. He slipped his fingers between the ropes and his brother to ensure the younger boy's comfort.

"We have a problem." Roark gestured at the window where a Guild gull squawked, with a Guild mission scroll tied to its leg.

"Hopefully, it's a small one."

Alana went to retrieve the scroll. It was Corwin. He had a job for a War Ender. Below the dossier, he had added a small note.

If you plan of keeping another apprentice, do not forgo this job.

Apprentices were so expensive. And one day, they would be the death of her.

✳

Elizabeth Guizzetti

ACKNOWLEDGMENTS

I am fortunate for the ability to pursue my passions--even when the first drafts don't turn out. The Martlet Series started out life as my second novel. Though I always loved the characters, I knew the original work had issues. Thankfully after being published a few times, I was able to look at the original novel with a more discerning eye. I realized the problem and broke the original manuscript up into novella sized chunks. The War Ender's Apprentice wasn't even in the original text, though it is based on a short story I wrote.

First of all, I would like to thank my darling husband for always believing in me.

I would also like to thank my editor, Joe Dacy III, and my proofreader, Cassandra Vaughn.

The War Ender's Apprentice would not be what it is without the help of my two first readers: N.D. Fessenden and Evan Witt. I would like to thank my writing group for believing in the project and to thank my friends at Two Hour Transport, since I started reading this novel aloud before it was edited.

I would also like to thank my fans who support my endeavors. Without you, none of this would be possible.

ABOUT THE AUTHOR

Much to her chagrin, Elizabeth Guizzetti discovered she was not a cyborg and growing up to be an otter would be impractical, so she began writing stories. Guizzetti currently lives in Seattle with her husband and two dogs. When not writing, she loves hiking and birdwatching.

Guizzetti loves to write science fiction, horror, and fantasy with social commentary mixed in – even when she doesn't mean it to be there. She is the author and illustrator of independent comics. She became a published author in 2012 and her debut novel, *Other Systems*, was a Finalist for the 2015 Canopus Award.

The War Ender's Apprentice is the first novella that Guizzetti has written.

Elizabeth Guizzetti

ALSO BY ELIZABETH GUIZZETTI

Comics published by ZB Publications

Faminelands
Out For Souls&Cookies!
Lure

Fantasy published by ZB Publications

The Grove

Science Fiction published by 48Fourteen

Other Systems
The Light Side of the Moon

Excerpt From

The Assassin's Twisted Path
Book 2: Chronicles of The Martlet

R OARK HAD NOT FORGOTTEN THE MAZE OF stone houses and neat hedgerows to the small cottage on the hill. Chamomile buds trembled in the windowsill concealing what lay inside the curtains. Roark dismounted and knocked on the heavy red door.

The lich peeked out.

"Hello, Master Candlewick. Do you remember me?" Roark asked.

"I don't think I could ever forget the taste of your blood, how is your aunt? Still chasing after worthless slaves?" Edar opened his door and motioned for him to enter.

Roark noted the new blue silk robes that hung on the lich's withered frame and wondered what Edar traded for it: a potion, a secret, another slave bled of their health? Inside, the reception room was clean, but Roark felt the oppressive nature immediately. He forced a smile. "We found Kian, but, yes, she is."

"Your aunt wastes her life on the unworthy. Please sit, my lad."

"I am Lord Roark now," Roark said, but he sat in the chair which Edar offered. "And Kian is my aunt's apprentice."

"How nice it must be for a slave to have a friend such as Lady Alana," Edar said.

Roark declined to answer the lich's needling,

especially since the undead human still followed the niceties of Dynion's northern providence. Edar set out bread studded with currants and put a pot of herbal tea over the fire. Chamomile and lavender by its smell.

"Your blood potion worked marvelously for healing. Wounds closed quickly, but the visual effects did not last," Roark said.

Edar poured him a steaming cup of tea and Roark took a sip, confident the lich wouldn't poison him since he cared so deeply for the bodily fluids of his person.

"Yes, and the healing is dependent upon the donor and the amount ingested. You are a fine donor. The potion made me appear alive for a hundred days. I even left the house several times."

"Alana sipped hers as needed, and she became a woman in her prime for a few weeks at a time. It was amazing." Roark chose his words carefully, "When we found Kian, he was quite ill. Alana gave him the rest of her potion. He completely recovered. That is why Master Candlewick, I want you to teach me. Necromancy is an exhilarating science."

"Not one condoned by the guild, Lordling."

Roark shrugged. "The Guild pays well, but the hypocrisies are many."

"Dangerous words." Edar pointed at the broach emblazoned with the golden bird holding Roark's cloak. "And that?"

"My mother still rules, my aunt still wanders, it will be many years until much is expected of me."

"Odd for a young man to care about necromancy. You're what? Seventeen?"

"Eighteen," Roark said. "I've seen death. I'll be killing another in three weeks. I don't want to see my end. Or Alana's."

"Alana fears death?"

"She doesn't fear anything, but she claims her

sword arm is slowing. Kian is to be her last apprentice."

Roark couldn't admit nightmares haunted him since Alana had decided to apprentice Eohan and Kian. He found happiness in their companionship, but he saw the deceit in common elfkin beliefs. The priests said if he lived by his vows, he would be resurrected as a Noblewoman's son. However, if two people as good-hearted as his friends might be born commoners and made slaves he no longer believed that a person's fate was anything but random chance.

A shadow of wretchedness drifted onto Edar's face, but it disappeared quickly.

"You obviously expect to come and go at your convenience?"

"The Guild's convenience, but yes," Roark said.

"What do I get from this arrangement?"

"I expected you shall want some of my blood."

"Yes." Edar smiled, exposing his yellowed teeth. "For regular donations, I will teach you everything I know. I won't bleed you too quickly. The one thing I have learned in my death is patience."

"Good. I'll need to water my horse and find her housing. Is there a nearer stable than the market square?"

"The mayor would be honored to stable a lordling's horse, but he'll ask your mother or aunt for a favor sometime." Edar gesture over his shoulder. "I keep a bed in my mother's old room. It needs airing, but its clean... and yes, lordling, there's a lock on the door."

Roark wasn't sure how Alana might feel about that, but he no longer answered to her. His mother and father needn't know or understand the risk.

"I'll return within the hour then, need anything from the shops?"

"The dairywife comes 'round in the morning, but if it isn't too much trouble..." Edar scribbled a list on a spare piece of parchment, and handed Roark a few coins.

"Buy some sausages or chops if any are fresh. It's been so long since I broke bread with another."

Taking the list, Roark rode to the mayor's stately house three streets away from Edar's little cottage. The mayor greeted him warmly, was glad to see Roark in good health, and inquired about Alana. He was thrilled to house an "Elf knight's horse" and offered to house Roark as well, but Roark declined.

On foot, the young lord did a turn about the shops, flirted with a rent boy and returned to Edar's cottage. The front door had been left unlatched for him. He set the fruit on the table, and meat on the cold box on the north wall.

"I'm here, Lord Roark."

Roark followed the voice to the rear of the house where Edar arranging lavender and wolfsbane atop an oak bed. He placed a crisp linen sheet over the herbs and mattress. "I hope you'll be comfortable."

The room was dressed simply, but well. Besides the oak bed, an oak chest lay on the east wall. Roark set his saddlebags on the chest. A washing pot was set on a small table, and a chamber pot was in the corner and had a folding door to the outside for emptying.

"A maid comes in on Tuesdays to keep the place neat. She will also draw baths but is not to be touched. She's a good servant and nurse when I need her to be."

Roark wasn't sure if Edar meant she wasn't to be harvested for blood or not to be molested but as the vows of his station and moral code prohibited him from doing either, he said, "I understand."

Edar opened the window and smiled sadly. "My mother had a nice prospect towards the garden."

When Edar spoke of his mother, Roark could almost see the man he once was.

"Like you, it was the aging of a beloved mentor which spiked my interest in necromancy. Do you need rest? I've much to show you."

"I can start immediately, if it pleases you, Master Candlewick."

"It does, Lord Roark," Edar replied with true eagerness in his voice and step. "But please call me Edar. Death has claimed many of my friends."

"Then please call me Roark as my aunt does."

Roark followed the lich down the cellar stairs to his laboratory. Heavy wooden cupboards filled with ceramic jars of organs, eyeballs. Empty beakers, scales, and ceramics of all shapes and sizes lined the east wall.

"You aren't squeamish?"

Edar lit candle lamps to illuminate the dead human corpse in the middle of the room on an iron table with a channel draining into a bucket below.

"No. My aunt bade me cut up many elfkin corpses so I'd know where organs are."

"Really? I've never seen the inside of an elfkin! Is that standard Guild training?"

"Only for surgeons, it's standard Alana training. Are all your specimens human?"

"Yes. This one was a thief, hung not two days prior. The mayor's man cut him down for the..." he gestured below his waist. "Male enhancements I could make."

"The mayor needs such things?"

"An old man hanging onto the breath of life needs many remedies. There are many remedies and poisons I can create from the pickled organs of an evil man. Come, I've so much to show you." Edar sliced off a piece of hairy flesh off the corpse and brought it to his stacked lenses on the north wall workbench. "Look, look at this."

Roark peeked through the lenses. It took a moment to clear his eyes, but he couldn't believe what he was seeing. Millions of tiny cells intertwined. "The skin doesn't look whole..."

"None of us are whole. I have seen my skin and

the slave boy. I rarely have an elfkin to experiment on. Kian was the last. I couldn't chance detection."

"I have a scar on my chest. I'll reopen it for you. Perhaps, I could bring you some subject matter from my travels. We could learn together."

Edar's eyes sparkled. "Yes, yes."

He walked to his cupboard and pulled down a jar of some unspeakable component, unable to stay still. "Roark will like this," he muttered to himself. "And this one." He returned, cranked the lenses higher in their base, and set the first jar inside and lifted the lid. "See this? It's a human liver."

A foul smell filled Roark's nostrils, but in the mass of decomposing flesh, the young man witnessed a world of heavy striations, circles and parabolas, and tiny dark specks that he could not see with his bare eyes. "Amazing. It's its own tiny Realm."

"Yes! My thoughts exactly. Would you like to see the human heart next?" Edar asked. "I can't wait to show you." He removed the liver jar and replaced it with another.

"Without the lenses, a human heart looks much like a Fairsinge or Daosith heart, but we have four large ventricles, not the two. I can't tell you where I'm bound, but perhaps if we study the differences between all intelligent species we might find the answers we seek?"

"Yes. How wonderful it'd be to study a vodnik, dwarf, telchine, or someone else. Bring back anything you can. How wonderful that would be!"

Edar clapped his hands together and went to the cabinet for another few jars, muttering about what Roark might like to see next as if Roark could not hear him.

He would have never guessed a lich might be lonely. That would be something he must plan for if he wished to live forever.

CPSIA information can be obtained
at www.ICGtesting.com
Printed in the USA
LVOW07s1525211117
557186LV00001B/193/P

9 780999 559802